IN GOD WE TRUST

THE JOURNEY OF JACK SAMPSON'S $1 AND $100 BILLS

Heather Hummel

© Heather Hummel, 2015

In God We Trust: The Journey of Jack Sampson's $1 and $100 Bills

Published by PathBinder Publishing

Printed in the United States of America

ISBN: 978-1519398727

First Printing 2015

Heather Hummel: www.HeatherHummelAuthor.com

Dedication

To Julie and Stephan

**Thank you for the cross-country journeys
and the tail wags along the way. You are my sunshine.**

Jack

1976

"*In God We Trust?*" Jack whispered.

Jack turned the one dollar bill over, looking at the front of it again. He noted the two long sets of dark green numbers and letters, an old man in the middle wearing a rather ugly wig, and the number "1" in each of the bill's corners.

"What's that mean, mister?" Jack flipped the bill back over and read out loud, as though in front of his fourth grade class, "*In God We Trust.*"

Jack held the bill out to the elderly man behind the counter in case the old man wanted a look for himself.

"What do you mean by *what's that mean*, son?" The clerk, who had just handed Jack the dollar bill along with a couple of coins and a brown paper bag filled with candy, peered over his glasses. "You mean on that dollar bill? '*In God We Trust*'? That's what you're askin' about?"

"Yes, sir. Why'd they put it on all these dollars?" Jack stood there, tapping his shoe against the base of the counter. He looked back up at the clerk, who had worked at the General Store for several decades before Jack came into the world.

"Don't know, son. Never gave it much thought. Now, you run along. I know that momma of yours is due home from work any moment. She'll be wondering where you've been, and Lord knows when she sees all that candy I let you buy, she'll be screaming enough."

"Yes, sir." Jack nodded and waved as he turned from the register. He pulled his ball cap down tighter on his head and ran out the door letting the bell hooked to the top of the door jingle loudly as he leaped down the steps and onto the sidewalk. Four blocks later, he made his way across the front porch and through the front door of the home he and his momma had lived in since his daddy died. Jack had just had his fourth birthday then. The years since had been hard on his momma, and most times even harder for Jack to understand. He could hear her crying herself to sleep at night, asking God why He'd left her alone at such a young age and with a boy to raise on her own. Jack would lie in bed, hands cupped together between the back of his head and the pillow, wondering why she thought she was so alone when his bedroom was right there next to hers. The walls were thin enough that it was almost like they were in the same room anyway. But, as she begged God to help her understand, Jack begged God to make it all stop, mostly to make his mother's pain go away.

The brown paper bag filled with one Whacky Pack, three gumballs, and a candy necklace for Susie, if he'd happen to see her, found its home under Jack's bed, but not before a handful of Jolly Ranchers were removed and shoved in his pocket by his dirty, sweaty hands. Back out on the porch, he sat down in a chair, swinging his legs and sucking on a grape Jolly Rancher. With care, he pulled the dollar bill back out of his pocket along with a thick, black ink pen he had grabbed from his mother's desk on his way out.

His grandmother in Michigan had included a five dollar bill in his birthday card. She began sending a card and one dollar for every year since his fifth birthday. Now that he was ten, she sent a five dollar bill. His mother insisted that he save half of it, and they agreed that he would store half of it in his piggy bank and he could spend the other half on candy or toys. The one dollar bill he held now was special to him, though. It was almost the Fourth of July, and the bill was a fresh 1976 one that he wanted to save. He looked down at it with a new found curiosity.

"Whatcha think that means, Jasper?" Jack reached down and pet the head of his neighbor's German Shepherd. Jasper always found his way over to visit Jack, especially when Sylvia, Jack's mother, wasn't quite home yet. "Here's what I'm gonna do, Jasper. I'm puttin' my name right above them words. That way everybody'll know that Jack Sampson trusts in God. That sound like a plan, 'ol Jasper?"

Jasper lay on the porch and thumped his tail while Jack carefully wrote, "J-A-C-K S-A-M-P-S-O-N" in the tiny space on the back of that 1976 dollar bill. His breath echoed each letter as he wrote them.

Jack had never seen, let alone held, a brand new dollar bill before—only the wrinkled and tattered ones that his mother brought home as tip money or that Blake Johnson would pull from his pocket at the Sunoco station to buy Cokes with. Blake was considered the neighborhood bully. Older than most of the kids, he ruled the streets. But, for some reason, maybe since Jack's daddy had died, Blake took a liking to Jack and never bothered him. In fact, he downright tolerated Jack. Even when Jack rattled off question after question about girls and cars and why they mattered so much to a boy Blake's age. Instead of swatting him away like a fly the way he did the other young boys, Blake sat Jack down and explained everything until Jack understood—or at least thought he did. Blake's interest in cars was always easier to understand than his interest in girls, but Jack listened to Blake's stories about both. Only once did Blake's dad overhear their conversation and yelled at Blake to "filter" what he told Jack, that he had some growing to do before understanding some things. After that, they took to whispering.

"There we go, Jasper. My name's right there on the back."

As Jack finished writing the N in the black ink on the bill, his mother pulled down the driveway in her 1965 Ford Galaxy. When Greg died, he left her just enough money to buy the car. Their old 1962 Chevy Impala's engine had blown the day after his

3

funeral. It was a beauty of a car though. Red leather interior and the outside gleamed with shiny red paint. They called it their "love-mobile." It was in the backseat of the Impala that Jack was conceived, and nine months later he was nearly born in the same spot. By the grace of God, they got to the hospital just in time. When the engine blew, Sylvia was convinced Greg took their love-mobile with him so she wouldn't be conceiving any more babies in the back seat.

Babies were the last thing from her mind as Sylvia drove down the driveway thinking about the Epson salt bath she'd be taking later that night. Her almost ten hour shift at the diner left her feet swollen and aching and her head heavy. Twenty-two dollars in tips lay on the seat next to her, close to her right leg. Not bad for a Wednesday, but for ten hours, it wasn't good enough. It never was, even with her minimum wage added to it.

Jack carefully folded his own crisp one dollar bill and put it in his back pocket where it was sure to stay flatter than a front pocket. Done with his Jolly Rancher, he folded its wrapper two times over and shoved that in his front pocket.

"What're you doing outside on the porch? Don't you have chores to do? Your room clean, Jack?"

"Yes, momma, it is. I've been wondering 'bout dinner."

"Brought you something from the diner. Go on in while I put my tip money in the jar. I'll be in the kitchen in a minute, and I expect that table to be set when I get there."

"Yes, ma'am." Jack opened the door, sure to hold it a second until his mother caught it with her fingertips. "Oh, and momma…glad you're home."

"Me, too, baby. Me, too."

4

Jack scrambled up the stairs and pulled the one dollar bill from his pocket. After looking around his room for a special place to keep it, he finally settled on carefully taping it to the roof of the inside of his top desk drawer. Anyone would have to stand on their head to see it. He knew it'd be safe there.

Sylvia

1976

"Time to get up, Jack! Your breakfast is on the table." Sylvia folded the top of a brown paper bag that held an egg salad sandwich and a chocolate chip cookie for Jack. She knew Mrs. Cooper would make him a hot meal and would have plenty of drinks, but by mid-afternoon Jack would be hungry for another snack. Sylvia didn't think it was fair that her growing boy would eat Mrs. Cooper out of house and home, especially since she took Jack in during Sylvia's shifts for so little money in trade.

"I'm ready!" Jack hustled into the kitchen. He held a baseball glove in one hand and a bat in the other.

"Put those in the car. You have your snack to carry, boy."

"Yes, ma'am." Jack ran out and dropped the baseball gear in the back seat. He loved going to the Coopers' in the summer. Mrs. Cooper had three boys of her own—John, Peter, and Chris, who was Jack's age. They welcomed Jack like a fourth brother, and the four of them played baseball and swam in the river till their skin was tanned and their clothes tattered. One shake of their heads after an afternoon of baseball left dust cloud halos swirling high above them. If they rinsed off in the river, he was fairly cleaned up by the time Sylvia arrived to pick him up.

"You ready?" Sylvia came downstairs. Her hair was pinned in a bun on top of her head and her uniform was freshly ironed. She had two of them and they were in a constant cycle of being washed or worn. Her name tag, which was starting to fade, was pinned above her left breast.

Moments later Sylvia and Jack headed down the driveway in the Galaxy. A slight rattling noise came from the engine; it had been doing so for a while now. Sylvia was saving her tip money so she could get it looked at. The last thing she needed was more car trouble. In the meantime, she kept driving it, praying each time that the old car would get her to work.

As they rattled into Mrs. Cooper's driveway, Sylvia said, "I'll swing by and pick you up on my way home. You listen to Mrs. Cooper and behave yourself."

"I always do, Momma. She's never told you otherwise, right?"

"I know. You're a good boy, Jack. Don't forget we have the fireworks tonight. It's the Bicentennial, so they should be extra special."

"I'll be ready. Bye, Momma." Jack climbed out of the car, baseball gear and brown paper bag in hand. He started down the driveway, then stopped and ran back to the driver's side window, leaned in and gave his momma a kiss on the cheek.

"Love you, boy," she said.

"Love you, too, Momma. See you later." As he ran toward the Coopers' front door, the three boys poured out of it calling Jack's name and slapping him on the back as they greeted him.

As she backed out of the driveway, Sylvia waved to Mrs. Cooper who stood in the doorway wearing an apron, a long skirt, and tennis shoes.

The diner was just over a mile away. Sylvia started working there only a few months after burying Greg. In some ways, life at the diner saved her own life. Busying herself by smiling at customers, taking orders, checking on drink refills, and tending to the register when needed, kept her mind off all the *what ifs* and sorrow that would normally have invaded her space under the circumstances. By nighttime when she finally lay her head down and feet up, she was too tired to think. That didn't mean the tears didn't come. They did. She just didn't allow herself to think about the reason why. Most nights she cried herself to sleep with questions to God mumbled in between tears, and she woke up the next morning not knowing what her last thought was the night before or if she had dreamed at all. Ironically, it was pure exhaustion that kept her alive.

The Fourth of July holiday traffic heading to Chicago for the Fourth of July festivities had started a few days earlier, making the parking lot at the diner already packed when she arrived. She parked the Galaxy under a large oak tree in the shade and at the far end of the lot so her seat wouldn't be scorching hot when she left for home. People were coming and going through the front door, letting her know the early shift was as busy as expected. Since Greg's passing, holidays had the tendency to heighten her awareness of couples holding hands, fathers helping their sons put their coats on, and the sound of cars pulling out of the driveway with laughter and chatting families as they talked about their journey ahead. Their conversations would play out in her head the rest of the day as she went from table to table delivering meals and smiles to the next group of patrons.

Not many people actually stayed in Pontiac on vacation; the patrons were often people just passing through on their way north to Chicago or south toward St. Louis. But, Pontiac's diner, named Sal's Diner after the owner, was known for being one of the best of the best on Route 66. Their burgers were noted as the thickest and juiciest for hundreds of miles and the waitresses for being extra attentive and friendly. All the reviews said so. Sal's special recipe for the burgers was just subtle enough that no one could figure out the key ingredient. His wife, on the occasions when she came into the diner, would shake her head and say, "I no know!" to anyone who asked. She spoke little English, but those words she had perfected. Everyone knew not to even bother to ask Sal. He came in every morning before the sun even thought about rising and prepared the hamburger patties himself. This meant his employees could never be held liable for letting out his secret recipe. The mystery was just as intriguing to them, so much so that they proudly told customers and begging reporters that even they didn't know the secret.

"Can't you check the food inventory?" a reporter once asked Sylvia.

"Well, no. Other than the meat itself, he brings the ingredients from home each day and takes them with him each night. They're under lock and key the rest of the day." The reporter shook his head, unsatisfied with her answer, but not surprised either.

"Sylvia, grab table four, will you?" Sal bellowed at her from in the kitchen when he saw her pass through the door. The smell of bacon, eggs, and coffee filled the restaurant.

"On my way!" She hung her sweater on a hook in the backroom, grabbed her apron from a cubby, stuck a pencil behind one ear and kept another in hand with her pad of paper for taking orders.

"Good morning. Welcome to Sal's," she said as she approached table four, where she was greeted with a family of four. The father sat on one side with their son and the mother sat on the other side with their daughter. That scene would have caused her to cringe in years past, but now she smiled, took their order and chatted an extra moment with the kids. Kids always took to Sylvia. The fact that she looked a little like Olive Oyl gave her a special caricature look that put them instantly at ease, as though she might just be Olive Oyl come to life to bring them their meals.

"What brings you through Pontiac today?" she asked.

"Traveling down Route 66. Heading southwest," the father said. He glanced up from his menu, smiled at her and placed orders for the entire family. His wife and kids seemed used to this, and simply nodded with a smile when he pointed at one of them and stated what they'd be eating.

"Well, you've come to the right place to fuel your bodies for a long drive! Your breakfast is comin' right up. Just remember that I'm Sylvia, and you let me know if you need anything. You kids see if you can finish those mazes on your menus before your food gets here. If you do, I'll give you a candy for the road. Of course that's if your daddy and momma will let you have it."

"Oh, they will!" the boy answered. His crayon was in hand and already following the black lines on the paper. His sister just sat and stared at Sylvia. Probably trying to figure out which cartoon she knew her from.

Sylvia moved over to the counter where Frank, one of Sal's oldest customers, was sitting. And by old, he was not only the first customer to be served, but he really was the oldest. His last birthday party, his ninety-second, was held right there at the counter. His wife and most of his friends had long since passed and everyone at Sal's had become his family. He had blown out his candles through the hole in his smile where two of his teeth used to be. Everyone in the diner got a piece of cake that night and Sylvia brought one home for Jack; Sal was always real generous about letting her take food home to Jack.

"Mornin', Frank. What'll it be today?"

"Lordy, Ms. Sylvia, you know this old man doesn't have the notion to change his underwear most days, let alone what he's gonna to eat for breakfast. Gimme my usual."

"Thanks for that thought, Frank." She scribbled his order and stuck it on the clip above the window to the kitchen. "Sal, Frank wants his usual." She always made a point to voice Frank's order to the kitchen; it made him feel important. Most times they were the first words she said to Sal in the morning.

When the meals for the family of four were ready, Sylvia stacked the plates on her arm after stuffing a bottle of hot sauce in her apron pocket and made her way back over to their table.

"Look! I finished the maze before you came back! That means you owe me a piece of candy." The boy's grin was wide as he held up the paper placemat that displayed his well-lined maze, strategically lined in purple crayon.

"Jack, that's rude!" the father scolded.

"Oh, it's okay. A promise is a promise, and I'll get you your candy as soon as you eat all of your breakfast because I know your daddy and momma wouldn't want it any other way." Sylvia put the plates down in front of each of them. "And, guess what? My little boy is named Jack, too. You've got a special name."

"Really? How old is he?"

"He just turned ten." Sylvia put the hot sauce on the table.

"I'm eight. Named after my daddy. Is your Jack named after his daddy, too?"

"No. No, he's not. His daddy was named Greg." Sylvia looked at the father, "Anything else I can bring you?"

"No, I think we're good," Jack senior said. "Umm, I don't mean to pry, but what did you mean by 'was named Greg'?" He twisted off the top of the hot sauce as he looked up at Sylvia.

"Jack, that's none of your business!" his wife exclaimed. "Pardon my son's *and* my husband's rudeness, ma'am." She looked apologetically at Sylvia.

11

"Oh, it's okay. My husband, well, he died real sudden when Jack was just four years old. But, we're doing all right. Jack's a good boy. Looking forward to seeing the fireworks tonight. You kids going to see them, too?"

"We sure are, right dad?" Jack junior said.

Jack senior patted his hand on his son's arm to temper the boy's excitement. "We'll find somewhere, son. Lots of places along Route 66 ought to be having them."

Jack junior held a fork in one hand and a knife in the other as he battled his way through his pancakes. His sister still did not say a word. Between bites, she glanced up at Sylvia with her mouth slightly ajar, if not chewing.

"I'm sorry about your loss. You're so young and pretty. What a shame, really a shame," the wife said. Jack senior nodded in agreement. His mouth was full, but his expression was one of sympathy.

"It's okay, really. We're doing just fine. Just fine. Now, if you don't need anything else?"

"The food looks great. Thank you," said the wife.

Sylvia had grown accustomed to customers asking about her family, and occasionally having to explain that she was a widow at an age when life was supposed to be beginning. She missed Greg even more on special occasions and holidays. The loneliness brought out pangs of depression she normally only felt in the dark, coldness of her bedroom. Though the pangs waxed and waned, they lingered with her throughout the day. Even though it started to grow easier with time, answering well-meant questions was especially difficult around the holidays, which brought out families by the dozens. The rest of the year their patrons were truck drivers passing through on their cross country routes and the elderly locals. They were the ones who came through the front door and filled the seats with their usual orders about 350 days a year.

"Sylvia? Did you hear me?" Sal called from the kitchen.

"No, what?"

"Come back here a minute."

Sylvia tightened her apron string as she walked around back to the kitchen and stood by Sal as he flipped an omelet.

"You keep that pretty smile on your face, you hear? That's what the customers come in here for."

Sometimes it was hard to tell if Sal was protecting her or prodding her. She always took it as his gruff way of watching out for her because she simply couldn't handle it if he was being controlling. After as many years as she'd been there, that fine line was never talked about. It became their silent language through which she'd come to find comfort. He was old enough to be her father, but she related to him more like an uncle.

"Yes, Sal. I know they do. My smile and your cookin'." She turned and left, waving her hand to let him know she had it covered, and went back to check on Frank and to clear table seven before heading back to Jack and his family.

Several minutes later, Sylvia could see that their plates were clean as she approached their table once more. "Here's your check, unless there's anything else I can get for you?" Sylvia said to Jack senior, placing the bill on the table in front of him. "And, here's the candy I promised both of you." She handed a gumdrop to each of the children.

"Thanks!" they both said, looking at their parents for approval to eat them, which they got.

Jack senior pulled out his credit card and slipped it in the plastic slot of the black, faux leather billfold. "Any idea where we might be able to catch the fireworks later?"

"St. Louis is just about three hours from here. I hear they have fireworks over the river," Sylvia said.

"That would be lovely," Jack's wife said.

"I'm sure they'll be spectacular this year. Let me get this finished up for you so you can get back on the road. You still have a ways to go." Sylvia took Jack's credit card and returned a few minutes later with his receipts. "Thank you for stopping in. Enjoy your trip."

Sylvia placed the billfold on the table and smiled at Jack and his family before leaving to take Frank his bill.

"Not free today, Sylvia?" Frank grumbled. He swatted at a fly that had found its way in through the door.

"Take it up with the boss, Frank." Sylvia flashed a smile at him and gestured toward the kitchen were Sal waved between flipping eggs.

After Frank handed her a twenty, Sylvia went to collect his change from the register. When she returned, she left the bills and coins on the counter next to him as he sat and milked the last inch of coffee in his mug.

When she looked over at table four, Jack and his family had already left. The bill's leather billfold sat in the middle of the table with the receipt sticking out. It wasn't unusual for customers to sign their receipts and slip out before she returned, especially when it was so busy. She walked over to the table, picked it up and opened the billfold to retrieve the receipts. That was when a one hundred dollar bill slipped out and floated down to the table.

"What the...?" Sylvia picked up the hundred and looked closely at it. It was indeed a one-hundred dollar bill and as clean and crisp as could be. Customers never paid with a hundred dollar bill, let alone tipped one. In fact, she had never seen one before now, let alone held one. But, what was it doing falling out of the billfold? When she looked out the window for Jack Senior, she spotted them in their Mercedes sedan pulling away, leaving only the slight glare of brake lights as they momentarily stopped before turning Southwest Route 66.

Sylvia, at a loss for what to do or say, sat down in the booth and looked at the bill again. "Well, I'll be..." she whispered.

"Whatcha got there, Sylvia?" Frank called.

"Nothing, Frank. You need more coffee?" Sylvia called over her shoulder.

"No, I'm good. Gotta get going and start my day."

"Have a Happy Fourth, Frank."

"You, too." Frank slipped off his stool and headed for the door.

Sylvia picked up the billfold once more and on top of the credit card slip she found a business card with ink markings on the back. Realizing it was a note, she flipped it over and read: *Sylvia, Buy something nice for you and Jack. Happy 4th of July, Jack and Family.*

She tucked the card into her pocket with the one hundred dollar bill, looked out the window at the sky and whispered, "Don't know what I did, Lord, but thank you. Thank you, Jack and Family, too. Now, maybe now, I believe in angels."

The clatter of silverware on plates, voices both hushed and loud, and the motion of customers coming and going sang the song of Sal's Diner until closing time. Sal closed early on the Fourth of July so everyone could enjoy the fireworks, most especially this year—the Bicentennial.

*****

When Sylvia arrived at Mrs. Coopers, the boys were out in the yard taking turns swinging on an old tire hung on its ancient rope. Jack ran up to the car to greet her. "We going now, Momma? We going to the fireworks now?"

"Almost Jack, almost."

Mrs. Cooper waved from the steps as Jack climbed in the back seat.

"Thank you!" Sylvia shouted to her through the open window. "See you tomorrow."

Mrs. Cooper waved back and called her boys inside.

"These are gonna be the best fireworks ever, huh, Momma?" Jack bounced in the back seat.

"Yes, Jack, they should be. We've gotta go home and clean up first." Sylvia kept one eye on the road and one eye on her purse that contained the hundred dollar bill and her other tip money.

For the first time in years, Sylvia didn't put all of her tip money in the glass jar when she got home. Instead, she placed the one hundred dollar bill in her sock drawer, carefully rolled up on the inside of a pair of brown wool socks that had been Greg's. She laid Jack's business card with the note next to it. The Galaxy needed work, and being a priority, that was where the money would go. Blake's father turned the best wrench for miles, and she would take the Galaxy there first thing in the morning after dropping Jack off at the Coopers.

Sylvia looked in the mirror above her dresser. For a twenty-nine year old woman, she had age lines that wouldn't normally emerge until forty. She didn't care though. Her hair was long and auburn, but only spent a few hours a day down, and that was mostly while she slept. Sal was right. It was her smile that brought customers back again and again. Somehow she figured out how to smile through the pain, and no one was the wiser.

"Ready, Momma?" Jack stood at the door, hands in pockets.

"Sure am, Jack. Let's go see some red, white, and blues light up the sky!"

The park in the town square was crowded with locals, as the tourists had made their way on to their final destinations and probably bigger fireworks. But, Sylvia and Jack lay on a blanket and watched Pontiac's fireworks belt out brightly over their heads, cracking and pounding with each display. Sylvia glanced over at Jack's precious face as he looked on in awe. That night Sylvia slept soundly for the first time in a long while.

*****

"Blake's dad is gonna put new brakes in the Galaxy today," Sylvia said to Jack as they drove toward Mrs. Cooper's.

"That's great, Momma. They've squeaked for a while now, huh." Jack unfolded and refolded the top of the brown paper bag that held his lunch, a peanut butter and jelly sandwich on squished white bread that the jelly would soak through by the time he'd have his hands wrapped around it.

Even though Mrs. Cooper didn't hardly charge Sylvia what she was worth, it was still enough that it made a financial difference at the end of each summer month. When school started in the fall and she didn't have to pay Mrs. Cooper, tourist season would be dwindling and so would her tips. Somehow it all balanced out, but it was rare that she was able to get ahead. For now, the one-hundred dollar bill she got from *Jack and Family* was pressed in her wallet between a few twenties. She'd be giving it to Blake's dad when the car was ready later that day.

"Okay, you be good! I'll pick you up this evening." Sylvia pulled Jack's head to hers and kissed him on the top of it as he climbed out of the Galaxy to greet the Cooper boys. She loved the smell of his freshly shampooed head. The smell always stayed overnight, only to be lost to sweat and dirt by the end of the day. But, in the mornings it was still fresh and clean. On the rare occasion when he'd been sick or if it was simply too hot in the house and he sweated during the night, the smell faded. But, most mornings the kiss she left on top of his head was the moment she cherished. The little things.

As she pulled into the local garage where Graham turned his wrenches, Sylvia felt only relief that she could now afford the brakes the Galaxy so desperately needed. Blake looked enough like Graham that anyone could tell they were father and son, but because Blake was growing and changing every day, there were times he looked more like his mother. Graham was solidly built and handsome under the grease and grime...or perhaps because of it. His demeanor made locals feel comfortable leaving their cars in his hands and knowing he wasn't out to fool anyone into expenses and fixes they didn't need. He was honorable and everyone knew it.

Blake's bad rap for being a bit of a bully came from his size and age. He did have a habit of using it to his advantage, but never had he actually hurt or threatened anyone. Graham probably had something to do with that. He kept Blake busy in the garage when school was out. There was always plenty for his son to do—ordering parts, filing invoices, calling customers, and running out to pick up parts when they couldn't be delivered. The day

Blake got his driver's license, Graham sent him out picking up parts, thankful to have a new assistant.

"Well, there's Ms. Sylvia. Ready for those brakes?" Graham wiped the grease off his hands the best he could. Even though he rarely shook hands with customers, he still had the habit of wiping his hands clean when someone walked in.

"Yes, thank goodness. Literally. Because of the goodness of a family passin' through town, I can get brakes. Funny how God sends us angels, huh?"

"I imagine you have plenty of angels around you. We'll get your car set for you. Need a ride to work?"

Sylvia nodded yes; she hated being late.

"Blake! Come give Ms. Sylvia here a ride to work!"

Blake came from around the corner a moment later and led her to the old Ford pickup out front. He held the door for her while she climbed in and they rambled down the road to the diner.

"Thanks, Blake. Tell your dad I'll be back after work."

"Yes, ma'am."

Sylvia climbed back out of the truck and headed inside the diner. She pulled the one hundred dollar bill from her wallet and put it in her apron pocket. No way was she going to let it out of her sight that day. Even though she'd left her purse in the back of the diner for years without a problem, she wasn't taking any chances. At least a few times an hour, her fingertips instinctively reached into her pocket and felt for the bill.

When Sylvia's shift finally ended, Francis, another waitress, gave her a ride to the garage.

"It's all fixed, Ms. Sylvia." Graham handed over the keys to her car. "I did an oil change and a few other tweaks for you, too. Able to keep it in your budget, and knew it needed it."

"Thanks, Graham. What do I owe you?" Sylvia tugged at her wallet in her purse until it came loose.

"Seventy three today." He handed her a printed receipt showing the work done.

Sylvia handed him the one hundred dollar bill and three singles, to which he handed her a twenty and a ten in return.

"Drive safely," he said.

Sylvia climbed in the car and began her drive to Mrs. Cooper's.

Stan

1984

In the late summer months, as school was starting, the sun reached Jack's bedroom floor by noon and then his bed shortly afterwards. For now, his small, wooden desk, which sat in the corner, absorbed the bulk of the morning sun. The lamp's shadow made its way slowly across the top of the desk as the hours passed and noon arrived. The desk itself was covered in Wacky Pack stickers. He had started with "Cap'n Crud" and from there his collection grew. Soon enough, the stickers took over every flat surface from every angle. One of the neighbors had given the desk to Jack when he started first grade. Knowing he'd have homework and he'd need it, Sylvia was grateful for the gesture and Jack loved all the drawers, more places to put stickers.

"Jack! The bus'll be here in fifteen minutes. You've gotta eat, and you can't be late on your first day."

"Coming!" Jack yelled as he ran down the stairs. His navy blue backpack held his biology, geometry, and social studies books.

"Now, be respectful to your teachers. High school is different. Teachers expect more from you."

"I already know most of them." Jack's backpack landed with a thud on the counter.

"Even so." Sylvia stood by the refrigerator with her hands on her hips and her hair tied up in the same neat bun she'd worn every day for years. "Do you want to take lunch or buy it?"

"I'll buy. I have a five."

"How're you going to keep up that paper route this fall? Getting up so early when you're up late doing homework?"

"Let me try it for a while, okay? You know we need the money." Jack pulled his PopTart from the toaster, poured a glass of orange juice, and sat down to eat.

"We'll see, but if them grades of yours start slipping, you've gotta give it up. Oh, and don't forget Stan is picking up your desk this afternoon for the church bazaar. You emptied it, right?"

"Yes, ma'am," Jack drank a sip of juice. "I'll put it on the front porch for him so he don't need to bring it down the stairs."

"That's my boy. Now finish eating." She kissed him on his forehead, even though he had to bend down now for her to do it.

After the last bite of PopTart, Jack brought his childhood desk down the stairs, careful not to bump the wall or the railing. Sylvia propped open the screen door. "Put it at the bottom of the stairs for him," she said.

Jack placed the desk where his momma said to, and then ran inside to grab his backpack.

"See you later, Momma," he called as he ran down the driveway to meet the bus.

That afternoon Stan, one of the neighbors who volunteered for most of the church fundraisers, came by and picked up Jack's old desk. He readily found it at the bottom of the steps and carried it across the yard to the driveway. As he loaded the desk into the back of his pickup truck, the top drawer slid open, exposing the still crisp one dollar bill Jack had written his name on eight years earlier. Stan slid the drawer closed, not noticing the bill. After a few more stops and forty minutes later, he arrived at the church where he unloaded the desk and the several other brick-a-brac items. A team of organizers helped him sort through the contents of his truck, separating them into areas of the large storage room next to the church's back door. Once he placed the desk in the back corner, smaller items were set atop and around it. All of it would be price tagged and spread out on the church's lawn that Sunday.

The day of the bazaar was a cold and rainy early fall day. The turnout was as miserable as the weather, leaving many of the items at the church. The few volunteers stayed that afternoon and placed the remaining items back in storage.

"I hate to see this desk go to waste. Certainly one of the kids in the congregation could use it?" Stan said to Linda, another volunteer, as they stacked boxes.

"Maybe Ms. Rachel's child could use it. From what I hear, that boy needs some discipline when it comes to school. A desk with stickers might just keep him in his seat!" Linda said.

"Good idea. I'll ask her during service tomorrow," Stan said.

After all the volunteers left, Stan moved the desk to the front of the storage room just in case Ms. Rachel did want it. He could deliver it to her after church. As he pushed it against the wall by the door, the front legs stuck to the floor, pulling the desk forward and causing the drawers to slide out; one of them landed on the floor just inches from his foot. As he leaned down to pick up the drawer, he noticed the green and white paper stuck to the roof.

"Well, what do we have here?" As he carefully peeled the bill from the roof so as not to tear it, he examined it. "JACK SAMPSON. Well, Jack, looks like you forgot to empty the desk completely."

Stan went inside the church's office, picked up the phone book, and dialed the diner.

"This is Sylvia?" She couldn't imagine who would be calling her at work.

"Sorry to bother you, ma'am. It's Stan from the church. I was going through the leftovers from the bazaar and found a one dollar bill stuck in Jack's desk. Do you want me to bring it by?"

"Oh, Stan. That's sweet of you to offer, but don't worry about that. Please just put it in the tithing basket on Sunday. I have to work, so I won't be in. You know how it is with the diner's hours."

"Yes, ma'am. And thank you. I'll sure do that."

Stan hung up and the next Sunday morning JACK SAMPSON's still crisp one dollar bill, now eight years old, was the first to land in the tithing basket during service. Stan made sure of it. The bill lay on the bottom where other bills, checks, and envelopes piled up on top of it.

Christopher

1986

Christopher Leake's 25,000 square foot home on Georgica Pond in East Hampton hosted the most sought after Labor Day weekend poker game. Players had to be invited, and only when one member moved too far away or died would their seat at the coveted table become available. There were a few, over the years, who moved and yet still returned for the weekend, no matter how far away they lived. Their in-demand seat on an auction block of popularity was not one any of them was willing to surrender.

Spending a weekend at Christopher's estate was worth the invite alone. The mystery of the card shuffling game, Texas hold 'em, and what went on at his estate and behind closed doors held questions and suspense to all who knew of the event but who weren't invited. Privacy was held to the highest standards by those lucky few who were invited, and it was just that intrigue that made outsiders want a look in...a peek through the window at the activity surrounding the hands played.

The sixty-eight inch, black diamond stainless base poker table sat in the middle of the game room. Each of the stainless cup holders held a bottle of Chimay Doree beer, though some were emptier than others. Christopher had been saving them for this year's tournament.

"Christopher, you pulled out the Chimay Doree for us?" Pete asked, then turned to Mack. "Think those Monks in Belgium noticed their beers are missing?"

25

"They're probably ringing the bell in the abbey right now. Calling in the townspeople to see who the heck's got 'em." Mack chuckled. Regaining focus on his cards, he bellowed, "Damn it, Pete, you're gonna go blind looking at those cards so hard."

The cigar smoke filled room went quiet as each of the men examined his own hand's worthiness while they waited for Pete.

"All-in!" Pete exclaimed. He had the most annoying tendency to go all-in early, a tactic that both worked and backfired, but always annoyed his opponents.

"For Christ's sake, Pete...or should I say, 'for Pete's sake'? Don't you have any other tricks up your sleeve?" Mack slammed his cards to the table. "Fold."

"You were right; it's for Pete's sake. Christ has nothing to do with him." Christopher mumbled. "Fold."

The others folded as well, and Pete collected the pile of cash in the middle of the table.

"Mercy, it feels stuffy in here," Christopher said. "Let me open the slider. Anyone need anything?"

After a round of "no's," Christopher rose from his seat and walked over to the slider. Mack stood up, grabbed a magazine and went to the bathroom. The others merely sat back in their chairs, awaiting the break's end, or stood to grab another plate-full of snacks at the buffet.

Christopher slid open the sliding glass door and stepped out into the cool night's air. The sensor light tripped on spotlights around his grounds, showcasing his well-manicured backyard and evergreens. Earlier that day he had reeled back the cover and left the lights on in the pool for ambiance, simply because he loved the way the water's ripples shimmy- danced over the lights' rays when the wind picked up. He took as much pleasure in looking at his pool as he did swimming in it. He kept it heated year round, just in case he had the urge to swim a few laps on Saturday mornings, the only day of the week he might.

Christopher's twin daughters, now grown and on their own, celebrated every single birthday party splashing in that pool, something his son missed out on by having a February birthday. Swimming helped ease the emotional blow the divorce took on him, so Christopher only started keeping the pool heated year round since the divorce. He found the surreal peace beneath the water to be comforting.

Now when his children came to visit, they only lounged around it, as though there was a statute of limitations on the age you could get your hair wet with chlorinated water.

"But daddy, I *just* had my hair colored last week! You can't expect me to get chlorine in it?" Lindley balked, as though chlorine may as well have been urine.

"No, darling, I can't imagine what chlorine could do to your already blond hair," he refuted.

"You just don't get it, Topher. Leave the girls alone." Their mother had sided with the twins on everything, leaving their son his only ally, and a weak one at that since he refused to get in the middle.

Now that his children were gone, and his divorce long settled after Gretchen left him for her painting instructor three years earlier, Christopher was adjusting to bachelorhood in his fifties. The house, the gardener, the maid, and the pool maintenance crew were his regular companions. The one thing that didn't change was that his workdays hadn't skipped a beat during all of the personal upheaval; he was still on the train bound for New York City by six a.m. and often didn't return home until after ten, when he took his nightly swim before bed. The hustle of the city blocks quite easily lured him away from the quiet walls of his home. However, his annual poker party was something he looked forward to hosting. The ritual weekend began long before the divorce, hence the table being set up in the basement. Complete with Hoyo de Monterrey cigars and dirty jokes that rivaled Andrew Dice Clay's, the game often started on Friday night and carried well into Labor Day Monday.

"Christopher, what are ya doing?" Pete called from inside.

"Coming!" Christopher left the door slightly open and headed back to his seat. "Who's deal?"

"Mack's," Pete said, sliding the disc in front of Mack and handing the stack of cards to Craig for shuffling.

The cards flew around the table, landing perfectly in ten piles. Hands swept them up and eyes took in the suits, each in hope of a playable hand. As the betting resumed, so did the tension. Stakes were high by time the flop round came, but when it came to the river card, cash was stacked higher than any other round yet.

"All-in," Mack said.

"For Mack's sake! It's okay when you do it?" Pete said, tossing his cards in the pile. "Fold." His fold was followed by the rest of the table and Mack took the pot.

The Texas hold 'em rounds carried on into Labor Day, after daybreak, after breakfast, and right up until lunch, when Christopher's final hand won him the largest pot of the weekend.

"Here ya go," Pete pushed the wad of cash on the table toward Christopher. "Thanks again for hosting."

"Sure thing. Next year?" asked Christopher asked as he began scooping up the bills.

"Hope so. We'll see what nineteen eighty-seven brings." Pete patted Christopher on the back and headed upstairs.

The rest of the men lined up in single file to thank Christopher and shake his hand. Though he was the host, they knew he had won fair and square, especially since he hadn't won in three years.

By the time each one left, Christopher had collected the entire stack of cash from the table, some of which would be spent on lunch and dinner in the city for weeks to come, depending on where he went and if he had a date with him. As he organized the bills, facing them Presidents' faces side up and in order of denomination, he came across a one hundred dollar bill with handwriting on it. On the left side of the steeple of Independence Hall it read JACK, and on the right side of the steeple, it read SAMPSON.

"Well, Jack Sampson, looks like I just met your Ben Franklin."

What Christopher couldn't have known was that Jack Sampson had pulled the bill from his momma's wallet and written his name on that one hundred dollar bill eight years earlier while his mother ran inside for her sweater that morning they took the Galaxy to have the brakes fixed. In her hurried state to pick up the car later that day, Sylvia never noticed Jack's name on the back of what had been her tip money from *Jack and Family* that turned into payment for car repairs.

"Did you say something, Christopher?" Mack called from down the hallway.

"No, Mack...just cleaning up. Thanks."

"Okay. Well, see you."

"See you."

Christopher took one last bite of pastrami before Sally, one of three maids he hired for the event, would bring the tray of leftovers to the kitchen. The cheese had been sorted through and was down to only a few slices. However, there were plenty of crackers, bread, and other assorted meats left. He knew the maids would pack up the leftovers and take them home. He certainly wouldn't be around during lunch or dinner meals to eat them.

Christopher placed the $100 bill with Jack's name on it back in the stack of plenty before setting aside more than a few of the other Ben Franklins for the maids as their tip for the weekend. The bill with Jacks' name on it made it into his pocket with the rest. Christopher went upstairs and fell asleep for the rest of the day and night. He didn't hear the help leave after cleaning up on Monday night, but awoke to the sound of birds chirping outside his window on Tuesday morning.

*****

Fall in Manhattan was Christopher's favorite time of year. Central Park boasted pathways of orange and red canopied trees. At night the lampposts lit the color infused canopies, casting shadows as the wind whipped through them, rustling the leaves. Christopher left a meeting in Lincoln Center and walked through the park toward Columbus Circle. He was meeting a dinner date on West 51st Street, a woman named Claudia whom he had met through a mutual friend.

Inside Le Bernardin, Christopher kept his hand on Claudia's back as he followed her and the hostess to their table. He had made the reservation a few days prior. The restaurant was new to the city, but had originated in Paris in 1972. Known for their seafood, he had been excited to eat there, and Claudia was just the right woman to bring. He had dated others since his divorce, the usual rebound type dates, but his friend was right, Claudia was different. A former opera singer, she radiated an elegance and class of an earlier era. He was originally struck by her blue eyes and the soft curls in her long brown hair. The manicure that punctuated her soft, warm hands as she reached out to shake his hand when they first met was only the beginning of the many qualities he would soon learn about her.

The hostess sat them, and in what seemed like only moments—because they were caught up in conversation—their dinner arrived.

"So, tell me, Christopher. How was the weekend of poker?"

"Oh, it was an eventful one. Let me show you something," he said. Christopher reached in his wallet and withdrew one of the one hundred dollar bills. "One of the bills in the pot had a name written on it," As he held it up, he read, "JACK SAMPSON. What do you think of that? He wrote it in all caps. Probably no reason, except it's a nineteen seventy-six bill. Makes it ten years old."

"I don't know. Let me take a look?" Claudia examined the bill. "It looks like he wants the world to know he had a one hundred dollar bill at one point. Or maybe he did it so if it ever came back to him, he would know it was the same one?"

"That's what I kind of figured. That he would want to know if the same bill came back to him, despite the ridiculous odds." Christopher took the bill back and stared at it for a moment.

"What are you thinking about? Finding Jack Sampson?"

"That would be nearly impossible with a name like his. John Smith, Jack Sampson, anyone with names like those would be too difficult to track. Just makes me wonder where he is though. When he wrote his name. That kind of thing. Kind of silly I guess; it's just a one hundred dollar bill with a name on it."

"Oh, I don't think it's silly. It's nice to wonder about where things came from, and perhaps where they're going." Claudia gave Christopher a wink and the twinkle in her eyes told him she wasn't talking about the bill anymore.

At the end of their meal, including the most decadent dessert on the menu, Christopher and Claudia walked hand-in-hand through Central Park in the unusually warm fall air. The next day, Christopher bought a new green tie at Hermes on Fifth Avenue and handed the Jack Sampson $100 bill to the cashier.

"Thanks for the tie, Jack. I'll think about you when I wear it, and I hope the Ben Franklin makes its way back to you," he mumbled.

"Excuse me, sir?" The clerk had returned from boxing and bagging the tie.

"Oh, nothing. Thank you." Christopher left Hermes's smiling.

Carrie

1987

Carrie finished her final lap around the Adlai E. Stevenson high school track just as her coach blew the whistle alerting the girls to hit the locker room. She grabbed her towel from the track's edge, wiped her forehead with it and picked up her now warm water bottle. As she walked toward the sidewalk that led to the gym, Carrie glanced around at her surroundings. It was early in the season and their coach was already running them hard, as evidenced by the group of red-faced, sweaty girls making their way off the track. They were expected to have kept up during the winter, even though Illinois wasn't known to be the best for running outdoors year-round. Snowbanks and the threat of frostbite saw to that. Instead, Carrie found her way to the downtown indoor track either before or after school, sometimes both. She went into the new season feeling prepared, except for one thing. Her Puma running shoes were at least two seasons old, going on three, really. The arch was wearing thin, not giving her the support she needed, and her toes were starting to poke through. There wasn't much she could do about it, though. Her father had lost his job several months earlier and new running shoes were not on the top of his priority list with what little unemployment money he had coming in.

Carrie began babysitting for the neighborhood kids on weekends, which allowed her to stash away some money. But by the start of the season, she hadn't been able to save up quite enough to buy the new Pumas she wanted. Though he never asked her to, Carrie gave her father over half of the money she made so he could buy groceries to put food on the table or gas to get her to track meets. It was just three days after Carrie's thirteenth birthday when her mother left them. Her mother's goodbye was heartless and Carrie and her father didn't talk about it, especially since he had lost his job. They had to sell their house and move into a small, two bedroom condo at the edge of town. But, they were hopeful that he'd find a new job soon enough, and that the speed of Carrie's lengthy legs would win her a college scholarship for track and field. Her race times were worthy of scholarships; she just had to stay healthy and focused, which included keeping her grades up. She'd always been a straight A student, and her father would not let her grades slip just because her mother had slipped out the backdoor. They never knew where her mother went, let alone the real reason why. A middle aged man in a suit delivered the divorce papers one day after they moved into the condo. Carrie had watched as her father signed them, but not a word was ever spoken between them about it.

Her parent's divorce was something Carrie didn't discuss with teachers or friends either, and especially the new neighbors who were more than curious as to why an older man and his daughter lived alone. But, as the best babysitter in the neighborhood, she took good care of their kids, and they didn't want to risk upsetting her and losing a valuable presence for their children. So, they didn't ask a lot of questions and some even gave her bonuses at Christmastime. Carrie knew they were watching though. They watched how she and her father interacted, likely seeking something, anything, amiss to gossip about, but they never got the satisfaction. Carrie and her dad had become a team, and they worked together to do what they could to get by each day.

Off the track and in the locker room, Carrie showered and changed quickly so she could arrive at the Jacksons' on time. It was a Friday night and they were going out for their usual dinner and a movie date. They were her favorite family to babysit for because little Noah was an easy child to take care of. He rarely argued and only fussed when he didn't feel well. At five years old, he behaved more like an eight year old. He brushed his teeth and put on his pajamas, usually Superman, by himself and only wanted a story read before he went to sleep, punctually at 8:oo p.m. That left Carrie a few hours to herself before Mark and Elaine would return home. She cleaned the kitchen, then did her homework so it would be done for the weekend. Sometimes she'd talk on the phone with Christine, a friend who also ran track and field. But, they only phoned each other if Christine was home and not out on a date. Occasionally Christine came home early from a really bad date and called Carrie to vent. Christine was much more advanced in the dating realm, leaving Carrie to live vicariously through her experiences. Regardless of their Friday night activities, the two usually ran together on Saturday mornings when Carrie would get the full scoop on the night before.

At 10:52 p.m. that night, when Carrie walked through the front door, she found her father in his recliner watching the evening news.

"Was he a good kid for you?" he called from the living room.

"Yes, daddy. Noah's a good kid. Got all my homework done, too," Carrie called back from the kitchen. "Want something from in here?"

"No, I've got what I need. Come watch the news with me."

"In a minute. I want to change." Carrie entered her bedroom, which was much smaller than the one she had in their old house. This one didn't have pink walls or a bunk bed. Instead the walls were beige like all the rest in the building and her bed was a simple twin one that had been in the guest room in their house. The bunk bed was the first item to sell in their yard sale, leaving her with the twin bed. That was the agreement with her dad—she would get the bed that didn't sell first. Bunk beds were in big demand in their old neighborhood of families. They were perfect for sleepovers; however, Carrie hadn't had a sleepover since moving into the condo. A lot of her friends' parents were leery of letting their child spend the night in the new neighborhood, and Carrie suspected it was just because her was dad there. Even so, she was often invited to friends' houses for sleepovers, but she only accepted if she wasn't babysitting. Earning money was more important.

Carrie pulled on her sweatpants and took the small wad of cash the Jacksons had given her out of the front pocket of her jeans, which she then hung in the closet. She was a neat freak, but not by nature. It started when she was six. She'd hide in her bedroom and hum while she cleaned to avoid having to hear her parents fighting down the hall or downstairs or, worse yet, in the driveway where neighbors could hear and watch them. She let herself believe that if she kept her room clean enough, maybe they would stop bickering. The bickering finally stopped, but not because her room was clean, but because she heard the final slam of the backdoor followed by her mother's final footsteps down the driveway. The start of the car. The engine noise fading as it disappeared one final time down the road. That was when the bickering stopped and the thick silence had hung in the air ever since.

Carrie spread the money out on her bed. She liked doing that—seeing all the cash in one place. There were two fives and three ones. Normally there would have been a third five instead of the three ones, but Mr. Jackson was two dollars short when he went to pay her. He promised he'd make it up to her next time. Carrie flattened the bills Presidential side up, then put one of the fives and two of the ones aside for her dad. The second five dollar bill sat to the right toward her pillow while she picked up the final one dollar bill. Spotting ink on the back side, she flipped it over instinctively.

"JACK SAMPSON? Well, I suppose I found your one dollar bill, Jack." She put Jack's bill with her own five dollar bill, and tucked them in her top dresser drawer with the saved money that would pay for her new Pumas.

"Here you go, dad." Carrie handed him the five and two one dollar bills.

"Thanks, honey. You won't have to do this for long. I'm going to make this all up to you. You know that, right?" Her dad's eyes glistened when he spoke. It was the same conversation they've had since they moved. She knew he hated living like this. She also knew it wasn't his fault.

It had been a month or so since Carrie stopped asking him about how his job search was going. She learned that lesson from a neighborhood couple who was trying to conceive. People would ask them month after month if they had succeeded, yet each month the couple shook their heads "no." Eventually people stopped asking and the couple moved to another town in another state.

Instead, Carrie sat down on the couch and watched the remaining minutes of the CBS news with her father. "I only need seventeen more dollars to get the Pumas. Should be able to do that in a few weeks as long as the Jacksons keep going out for their date night." Her father winked at her and at 11:30 p.m. when the news ended, he turned off the television. "You're a good kid, Carrie," he said and retired to his bedroom.

The next morning Carrie went running with Christine. Each breath as her feet padded the pavement was her only hope for a scholarship to college. She counted on it more than anything, and although she knew her dad would have a hard time with her gone, she also knew that the four years beyond high school would pay off, and that she would be able to really help to support him then.

"Where are you thinking about applying?" Christine asked.

"Villanova and Florida State. They have two of the best track and field programs. What about you?"

"Florida State and UCLA are my top two. I want to be warm!" Christine said.

"It'll come down to who gives me the best scholarship." Carrie stretched her t-shirt up and wiped the sweat off her forehead. "I worry about being too far from my dad though. We don't talk about it, but I know he's worried, too."

Christine stopped running and looked right at Carrie. "You have to have your own life, Carrie. I know how much you love your dad, but remember—he wants you to be happy. That's what will help him, you going out and making the best of your life. You inspire him, you just don't see it right now, but you will."

"I know you're right. It still doesn't make it easy," Carrie said.

"Oh, heck. Maybe once you're out on your own, he'll meet a great woman and find his own happiness again. You'll see. Just you wait."

They finished their last lap and sat in the grass, catching their breath. Carrie looked up at the sky, closed her eyes, and let the sun warm her face.

Three weeks later she had reached her goal to buy the Pumas. That Saturday morning after running with Christine, they went together to the running shop where she bought her size seven running shoes.

"Thank you!" she said to the clerk as she handed over all of the cash that had been in her top dresser drawer, including Jack Sampson's one dollar bill. Two weeks after that, she won their first track meet with the Florida State University coach watching.

Doug

1988

The firehouse was quiet for a Friday night in the fall, although, the fear of that one family who forgot to clean their chimney before stoking their first fire of the season loomed. There was one every season, and it always made the news, which in turn gave an influx of business to the local chimney cleaners. Even with the efforts to raise awareness, Doug had seen it over and over again in his twenty-seven years as a volunteer firefighter, and he knew it would continue even after he retired. It was just the nature of the business.

"Doug, you cooking tonight?" Captain Sands came into the break room where Doug was reading the paper.

"There's some chili in the fridge if you want some. Cooked it up last night." Doug turned the paper to the sports section, scanning the article on the Marshfield High School football team. Their season was always a big draw in the little coastal town of Coos Bay, Oregon. It seemed as if everyone in town had a son who played for the team or a daughter who was a cheerleader at one point or another. It wasn't a matter of if; it was a matter of what year. Doug had played his senior year, but a torn rotator cuff kept him from taking a full ride to the University of Oregon. It was a loss to both Doug and the Ducks, and one that he felt for years to come. But, firefighting filled a different type of adrenaline rush. The team comprised of the firemen who had formed a brotherhood and the opponent roared its hot breath against their faces and bodies until one defeated the other. In his nearly three decades, Doug had attended four funerals, three of which were fire related and the other a heart attack. The cloud of smoke that hung over the job was both literal and proverbial, but Doug tended to look around the cloud and into the faces of the families whose homes they saved or cats they rescued. The smiles and relief of neighbors, and in some cases families of the firemen, made it all worth it.

"Looks good; I think I'll try some." Captain Sands was standing at the counter with the container of chili open. He pulled a bowl from the cabinet and a spoon from the drawer and then piled several scoops into the pot on the stove. While it heated, he broke off two hunks of Italian bread from the loaf that sat on top of the fridge. When he was finished, he brought his food to the table and sat down next to Doug. "So, how's it feel? Last week and all."

"Feels strange," said Doug as he looked over at his jacket and hat on the rack near the fire trucks. They were a bit worn and tattered. The fundraiser that was in progress would raise enough money to replace them with new ones, but by then Doug will have hung up his for the last time.

Captain Sands broke his bread and dipped it into the steaming chili. After chewing for a bit, he swallowed and said, "Can't believe you're retiring before me."

"We all have our due time, Captain. Yours will be soon enough. I can tell you that once that day is on the calendar, well, it's just different. You watch as the days move along to the past while that one eminent day grows closer. You can't stop it, and you don't want to. It's a weird kind of limbo that life puts you in." Doug stood up and walked over to the refrigerator where he took out a Coke and popped it open. "It's like you're ready for what's to come, but what's going on now is still going on. You know?"

"I hear ya." Captain Sands pushed the now empty bowl of chili away from him, leaving room on the table to rest his arms. "We've got a great group of guys here. Coos Bay's finest. But, you'll be missed."

"Thanks, I appreciate that. And don't worry, I'll swing by. Maybe even bring some chili."

Just then Peter came through the door. He was a few years younger than Doug, but hadn't aged quite as well due to the too many Budweisers he drank on his days off. His belly had grown rounder in the past few years, and the gray hairs had multiplied. When Doug provoked him about it, Peter blamed it on the two teenage daughters he had that Doug didn't.

"I've got plenty else going on," Doug had said at least a few times as a retort. The truth was, he didn't really.

A bachelor by choice since the day his high school sweetheart left him at the altar, Doug had lived a quiet life between fires. His brotherhood in the department had become his family, which was why they were surprised he was retiring while he still had enough life in him. They all secretly figured his last breath would be on a truck en route to a fire or lying on a cot on the second floor. No one figured he'd hang his hat and jacket one last time on his own accord. But, Doug had another passion that the men didn't know about. The boats and docks on the bay had become more than just a pastime for him. They were the subjects of the canvas paintings he created in his garaged turned studio. Just a month prior, he went out on a limb and approached a gallery up in Portland about a possible exhibition. The director loved his work and offered him a show the next spring, which was plenty of time to create a themed set of work that would be new and fresh. He knew that preparing for the exhibit would take all of his focus and attention, and with something so big to look forward to, the timing seemed right for retirement.

"Your work is exquisite," Lisa, the director, told him on that Tuesday when he made the drive up to Portland. He brought five pieces with him to show her. The introduction had been made by a lady friend, Pamela, who was one of the few people who had ever seen his studio. Doug had converted his garage to a studio several years ago. Though he often took a canvas and easel down

41

to the boardwalk, he liked to put the finishing touches on back in the studio. It also served him well on rainy days and as a place to store his work. Pamela had stopped by to borrow his pressure washer, which was kept on one side of the studio with a myriad of other lawn tools. She hadn't been in the studio before, only the house for glasses of wine before they shared his bed until late at night when she would slip out and go home. Her surprise at the quality of his paintings became his gain when she called her friend, Rebecca, at the Top 9 Gallery in Portland. The gallery's name referenced the other nine galleries that had ranked in the top ten in the area, but of course, Top 9 Gallery was actually the best. Rebecca had named the gallery Top 9 when she first opened, so naturally she hadn't ranked yet. It was more of a statement, and it took a long while before people figured out the meaning of the name.

"Thank you. I appreciate that, and your gallery came highly recommended by Pamela," said Doug.

"Pamela has a good eye for talent. She's one of the few I trust when people refer an unknown artist to me."

That afternoon Doug and Rebecca signed the papers and his exhibit date was set. He drove home along the winding Oregon coast with a new outlook on life. That Thursday when he reported to the station, he gave his retirement notice to Captain Sands. Then, on his next day off, he took a canvas, brushes, and his favorite easel to the coastline. What took him by surprise was the new resolve he had for each brush stroke, the way he viewed the scenery before him, and the feeling that went along with the knowledge that this work would be shown in a Portland gallery. His breathing just about matched each brush stroke, and his eyes transitioned their focus back and forth between the canvas and the scene.

Six weeks later, Doug hung eight works of art in his gallery and invited Pamela over to view them. He wouldn't let her even have so much as a peek at any of them until they were finished; he wanted her to get the complete impact at once. She was only one step inside the studio when her breath caught her. "Oh, Doug. These are marvelous. Look at what you've done!"

As they stepped inside, Pamela carefully walked across the floor in her four inch heels.

"You like them? Really?" asked Doug.

"Of course! My goodness, just look at them. They're even more stunning than your prior work. And the nautical theme, it's brilliant for that gallery. Its competition tends to sport urban culture, so this will be a refreshing change."

Doug had chosen to stray a bit from his usual landscapes and focused on the finer details of the coast—the buoys, the dock posts, the ropes. The changeup had challenged him, but paid off with the results. It was as though another force took over and helped him to create from a new perspective. The doors had been opened to looking closer rather than at the big picture, and he took the liberty of walking through it.

"What do you think of this one? It's my personal favorite. The muse really hit me that day." Doug pointed to the fourth painting on the right. It was of a faded red life preserver hanging over the edge of a rail near the dock. The tip of a boat was to the left, but it was the life preserver that caught the viewer's eye.

Pamela stood directly in front of the painting, eyeing it for a long moment before speaking. "It's telling in so many ways. Because I know you, I see the metaphor."

Pamela was right. Doug found his paintings to be his own life preserver from the rest of his life. The faded one in the painting reflected his aging, retiring for that matter, and his love for the sea was represented in the backdrop. The railing in which the life preserver draped over held the energy likeness of his easel.

43

There were many times he hung an arm over the edge of his easel as he viewed a scene before putting the brush to the canvas.

"The exhibit is sure to be exquisite. I'm so proud of you," said Pamela.

"It wouldn't be happening if it weren't for you. I needed this or I never would have left my life and my friends at the station."

"When is your retirement party?" Pamela began making her way toward the door.

"This Tuesday night down at the station."

Doug held the door open for Pamela and as she walked through it, he noted her near perfect physique. If only he had it in him to give her what she needed, what she deserved.

"Well, I have a meeting to get to. Thanks for showing me your work. I really do love it, and so will Rebecca." Pamela gave him a kiss on the cheek as he hugged her goodbye.

"Thanks. I owe you one," he said.

Doug spent the rest of the afternoon cleaning up the studio. It was his ritual to let it get as messy as needed until a painting, or even a complete series like this one, was done. Once complete, he set out to de-clutter and organize the space for the next wave. Much like fighting a fire, he went in giving a project his all, his life's breath, and when the fire was out, he prepared for the next. He often thought about the correlation on the days they washed the fire engines. Engine number 11 was his favorite. The lines of the 11 reminded him of parallel lines that never crossed. That was how he felt in relation to much of his life. Everything was kept at an arm's length, never letting it grow so close it would cross his own line.

That Tuesday night was a night he had both dreaded and looked forward to for some time. He knew the men would go all out and throw him a party he would never forget, some of which was what he dreaded. He had been to enough of the other men's retirement parties to know they go all out. It was how the brotherhood operated. What the men didn't know was that Doug had a gift of his own to leave them with.

"Oh, geez!" Doug exclaimed as he walked into the station that night. Streamers and banners he had expected, but the two girls dancing on the fire poles was a new one. Probably because all the other retirees had been older than Doug when they retired, and very married to wives who wouldn't have approved.

"Dougie boy! C'mon in!" Captain Sands called from across the room. The rest of the men stood and applauded Doug as he walked across the room to shake Captain Sands's hand.

Doug refrained from choking up, as he knew the toasts later would do that. "Okay, okay. Let's get this shindig started. No need for all the fuss."

"It's your night, Doug. Settle in and enjoy it," Peter called from across the room. The girls had stopped dancing for the moment. Doug smiled at them, but not too much to encourage them.

The food and drinks spread across the table were enough to feed three dozen firefighters, let alone the just over a dozen who were there. They lined up to fill their plates and cups, and when each one was seated, Doug looked around the room at the many faces that had been there for him over the years. Whether those faces were covered in soot or smiles, they were his family.

Charlie and Susan

1998

Pudley's, down the street from Stanford University, glowed with Christmas lights and bellowed with laughter. Cheers from inside could be heard out on the street, especially when a new patron swung the door open to join in on the celebration. The celebration was less about Christmas and more about Charlie. His dot com business just went public and his wallet was a lot fatter than it had ever been. Dropping out of Stanford in the midst of his junior year paid off. Not only his tuition for three years, but in, what he thought, every other area of life. He built his dot com business from his dorm room, and just hours before stepping up to the bar, he had put a bid on the house of his dreams in Palo Alto. The pool alone had his friends salivating and planning extravagant parties.

Most of the people surrounding Charlie were his Stanford classmates who had stuck it out for four years. They would graduate in the spring and begin the process of sending out resumes and practicing for interviews. They'd initiate e-mails to other Stanford alum in hopes for introductions to not the heads of human resources departments, but to the CEOs themselves. Meetings over coffee would be arranged as they would size one another up, mostly the CEO sizing up the recent graduate. But, some graduates would have their pick of jobs, salaries, and even benefits. Charlie's roommate, Hilton, would be one of them. Charlie and Hilton tolerated each other well because they both pulled early morning hours, Hilton studying and Charlie driving his business from nothing to a grand scale. His dot com focused on college sports; it was a sure hit no matter what part of the country a team played in. The big leaguers got behind Charlie. His God-

46

given talents helped—from his ability to smooth talk and an even better ability to spread a trusting smile from San Francisco to New York. In fact, he traveled often between the two cities, meeting with investors during the day and then spending nights celebrating a newly signed check with stewardesses he'd never call again.

The IPO launched earlier in the week, and the stock had already earned him enough money to set him up for life.

"To Charlie!" Hilton lifted his beer mug in the air, clanking it against the many mugs that had joined in. Strong pats on Charlie's back followed.

"It's on me tonight!" he called, smiling his famous smile as the cheers and pats escalated.

A moment later, Susan, his girlfriend during his freshman and sophomore years, entered through the door with a gust of wind behind her. The cool air felt good on the faces of those celebrating, but Charlie's face turned hot. Not with anger, but with passion.

Susan was the one who had ended it, and nearly two years later, Charlie still wasn't over her. All he had to do was take one look in her eyes or at her legs and he was lost. The whisper of her voice haunted him. What only he and perhaps Hilton, by observation, knew was that in many ways it was the loss of her that motivated him to start his company. The hours spent each night at the computer working on his business plan, researching the industry, and pitching his ideas to sponsors were quite simply an emotional escape. Never fully escaping, his work became more of a reprieve, like a cold 7Up on a hot day.

Now, watching Susan walk through the door, wearing of course a short skirt that showed her lengthy legs, punctuated with five inch heels, his heart paused. She paused, too, and looked around at the familiar and some unfamiliar faces. Then their eyes met. His frosted beer mug reached his lips, but the beer never made it to his tongue. Charlie had frozen. Not a sound was heard. Not a pat on the back was felt. Only the sound of his heart surrendering a loud couple of beats followed. She took a step toward him. He put his mug down. And without thought, he reached in his wallet, pulled out a wad of hundreds and lay them on the bar for the bartender.

"That ought to cover it?" he said. Without intent, he nodded at everyone and walked toward the door, brushing past Susan, who only spoke to him with her eyes. He thought they might have said, "Congratulations," but he only heard, "I don't love you."

The door closed and Charlie disappeared around the corner.

"You had to ruin it, didn't you? He was having the time of his life. What the fuck were you thinking coming here?" Hilton never held back when it came to Charlie, and especially when it came to Susan's influence on Charlie. He was the one who watched as Charlie lost fifteen pounds despite eating his way through depression. He sat with him silently as they watched Jay Leno on Friday nights, even though Charlie wasn't really paying attention to the guest of the night. He knew that Charlie wanted to marry her, and that she shattered that dream and his heart into a million pieces with those four words, "I don't love you."

"I didn't know. I thought..." Susan started.

"You thought wrong." Hilton reached toward the wad of hundreds Charlie had left on the bar and gave a look to the bartender that it was okay. There'd be enough left for him and the tab. He took one of the hundreds from the pile, looked down at it and said, "Here. This is to make sure you never come near Charlie again." He paused and looked down at the bill. "I hope you and," Hilton read the back of the bill, "Jack Sampson are very happy together. Now get outta here!" Hilton pulled five twenties out of his own wallet and put them on the bar nodding at the bartender.

"You ass..." Susan yelled, but not before Hilton made his way through the crowd and out into the cool air to find his friend. Her words were lost in the chatter that started again. She looked down at the hundred dollar bill in her hand and wondered who Jack Sampson was. It didn't matter though. Two days after she ended it with Charlie, she regretted it. But he wouldn't take her calls and slammed the door in her face when she'd stop by to try to talk. She thought his anger would dissolve, but it only seemed to escalate with each interaction, so she had stayed away for some time. But when she heard about his dot com success, and the celebration party, she thought maybe that would have softened him. Maybe he'd at least look at her. Neither had dated anyone else in the two years, which seemed ridiculous for college students, and the flight attendants he'd enchanted couldn't be considered dates. He was working and schooling eighteen or more hours a day, that was until he dropped out altogether. Then it was just work for eighteen hour days and a few hours of vegging with Hilton. Four hours of sleep had become his norm and most times he woke up in a cold sweat thinking about Susan anyway. His motivation to bury his feelings and build his business became his breath.

Susan folded the hundred dollar bill and tucked it in the outside pocket of her purse. She knew she wouldn't keep it. That would not only imply a promise made, but would satisfy Hilton. Christmas was just four days away. She was going home to Pasadena on the twenty-third to spend the holidays with her family. Her mother, father and sister Julie would be there. They managed to get together every Christmas even though Julie was studying at the University of Oxford. She was accepted on a full ride for surgical sciences. Susan was jealous that Julie got to go across the pond and experience a whole new culture, let alone the accents. But, Stanford hadn't disappointed her. She'd made great progress in her studies; her focus was on education with the hopes of teaching overseas one day. She just hadn't decided where in world she wanted to make a difference. Someone had suggested she look into teaching at a New England boarding school, saying that even the privileged kids needed guidance. The words echoed in her mind on days when saving the world seemed daunting. How nice would it be to spend the school year in a small, quaint New England town being challenged by intellectuals not much younger than her own years. She could arrange trips overseas in the summers, taking core students with her, and they could all make a difference together. Perhaps.

The bar door flew open, bringing in a cold rush of air like frozen dragon's breath that wrapped around Susan's back, which still faced the door. She didn't have to look over her shoulder. She knew.

"You!? How dare you, of all people, show up tonight!"

The heat of Charlie's words against the back of her neck thawed the dragon's breath and left it heated, even though she shivered on the inside. The first words he'd spoken to her in two years. Breakthrough.

"I...I just wanted..."

But he didn't let her finish. "Wanted to what? Keep ruining my life? Keep haunting me?" His words spit at her. "This was *my* night. You had no..."

"Stop it. Stop yelling at me. It's been two years. You think it's been easier on me? Well, Charlie, it hasn't! Not at all! But, you won't take my calls; you slam doors in my face. You won't listen to me." The tears that flowed down her cheeks were drawn from the two wells of love and frustration.

Charlie looked at her. She'd forgotten how dark brown his eyes were. How perfectly white the whites were. And how much she really did love him, despite her parting words their sophomore year.

"Can we go outside? Just for a minute?" She tried not to plead, but the eyes of the Charlie's friends around her were not friendly ones, and she was feeling like every beer mug, shot glass, and wine glass in the bar was about to empty onto her head. The ice and olives alone would be awful to endure.

No answer came from Charlie. Only a look of questioning. Susan grabbed his arm and gave him no choice but to follow her to the sidewalk. She had always been almost as strong as he was, but it never bothered him until now. Her days of rowing crew had paid off in upper body strength that most women didn't have, and still she maintained the grace and femininity that had first attracted him to her.

Once on the sidewalk, she let go of his arm since he hadn't put up a fight. Honestly, he lost the fight when she first walked in the door. The dichotomy of emotions of celebration and of seeing her only submerged his energy into the depths of his soul. He didn't know how to find his way back out. He'd surrendered even if he had given it one last try in the bar.

"What, Susan? What do you want?"

"Just for you to listen to me. Five, no three, minutes. Make that three words. *I love you.* I never stopped, but you were too stubborn to let me tell you." Susan's eyes pleaded with Charlie just as much as her words did. She waited for him to speak, but he didn't give her that. Instead he stepped backwards three steps and shook his head.

Susan pulled the hundred out of her purse. "This is what Hilton paid me to stay away from you. Nice, real nice, but guess what? I won't take it." She walked over to the bell ringing Salvation Army Santa Claus across the street. He hadn't stopped ringing the bell since they'd busted through the bar door and onto the sidewalk. His basket was filled with ones and fives, but when Susan reached him, she turned and held Jack Sampson's one hundred dollar bill and showed it to Charlie one last time before putting it in the basket. Santa stopped ringing his bell and looked at the cherry atop the pile below. He started to thank Susan, but she held her hand up to him. It wasn't his words she wanted to hear. Only Charlie's.

"There. Now you know my silence, my avoidance can't be bought. Love doesn't have a dollar sign on it, Charlie."

"You ended it. Not me. You said you didn't love me." Charlie surprised her. Though his words were angry, she knew the ice had cracked and the thaw had begun. She wasn't sure if she should let it go at that. Let him ponder all that she did and said tonight and trust he'd come back in his own good time. The other part of her wanted to run to him and hug him. He made the decision for her, though.

"Look, there are a bunch of people in there waiting for me. I have to go..."

"No, you're right. You should go back in. Thank you for listening, at least. But, Charlie, you have to know, that simply wasn't true. I was angry, but I was also wrong. Don't let your anger do the same. I'm only asking that you think about that."

Charlie started to walk back inside as Susan turned to walk away.

He turned around at the door and asked, "Can I call you?"

The sound of his voice cut through the ringing Santa's bells, the wind that whipped around her, and warmed her heart.

"Yes, I'd like that."

Charlie went back inside. Susan passed Santa and winked at him. Out of the corner of the basket she could see Ben Franklin's face looking back at her.

Samantha

1999

The image had been her favorite one despite the thousands of other photos she had captured over the years. It was taken with her Canon AE1 in 1985 on a trip to New York City. The construction workers were on their lunch break and readily agreed to her lens being aimed at them as they downed their Budweisers and took large bites of their pepperoni pizza slices. Her normally shy disposition transformed with the camera in hand, as though it gave her superpowers. When she later processed the film in her home darkroom, she smiled back at the faces of the gentlemen enjoying their meals. It was in that exact moment—as their faces appeared on the Kodak paper in the tray as she gently rocked it back and forth in the developer—when she knew she wanted to be a professional photographer. Now, fourteen years later, she had moved to Jackson Hole, Wyoming, and freelanced long distance with a New York City advertising firm as their go-to wildlife and landscape photographer. She had come a long way as a photographer, only now she was photographing the lakes and mountains rather than construction workers around the city. The views of the rugged mountainscapes through her lens had caused her to fall in love with Wyoming and its neighboring state, Idaho. Whether she was indoors processing film as the snow fell outside or outside on a trail hiking obscure trails near and around Jenny Lake, she was captivated. And, it showed in every one of her images.

It took time, but Samantha Sounder had become one of the most sought after photographers in the industry. From National Geographic to Time Magazine to the Nature Conservancy, and a multitude of smaller organizations, Samantha's proximity to one of the most beautiful spots in America combined with her exquisite photos kept her phone ringing on a regular basis. When she wasn't on a shoot, she was in her home office planning one of her own shoots or developing and processing her back stock of photos. When she wanted fresh landscapes, she took road trips to places even as far away as Oregon's Cascade Mountains and coastline, stopping on the way at places like Boise for its skyline and foothills backdrop, the broad-scoped Shoshone Falls, and the elegance of Sun Valley. She never tired of finding new places to explore and the Northwest had an unlimited supply. One day she planned on taking a trip to Montana to photograph cowboys on some ranches. She imaged the dust kicking up, their hats shading the sun from their faces, the strength of the horses. It all intrigued her.

Her images were becoming legendary for their rugged beauty and the way she knew how to subtly add a woman's touch to land that traditionally carried so much male energy. Sometimes it was a delicate flower in the foreground of a majestic mountain or the curves in the ripples in Jenny Lake. She would never believe that she had mastered her craft because every shoot brought new challenges. But, the reviews said otherwise.

In the privacy of her home, though, almost no one was privy to seeing her home office or that there was a 16x20 print of the New York City construction workers framed and hanging above her desk, providing her with daily inspiration.

It was an early Monday morning when her phone rang. Early wasn't unusual because people didn't always take her time zone into consideration when calling. On more than one occasion the answering of the phone was met with the caller apologizing and indicating they just realized what time it must be in Wyoming. On this day, however, it was unusual because it was July 5th and most people were taking advantage of the long Fourth of July weekend.

"Hello?" Samantha cradled the phone between her shoulder and cheek as she moved across the kitchen to grab the orange juice out of the refrigerator.

"Samantha, this is Don Peterson."

"Good morning, Don. What gets you up early this morning?" asked Samantha.

"Oh, I hope I didn't wake you?"

"No, not at all. I've been up. Can't capture those sunrise photos if you're not a morning person, right?" Samantha took the phone from her shoulder and held it in her hand now that the orange juice was on the counter.

"Right, hadn't thought that through, but it's kind of why I'm calling," said Don. "I have an idea to run by you. Do you have time for coffee or something later this morning? We could meet at Annie's Place. My treat."

Don owned the local frame shop in town and Samantha had done a lot of business with him over the years. Her curiosity was piqued. "Absolutely. I'm fairly free today because of the holiday. Is Annie's open?"

"Yes, I checked. She does a good business on days like today with people driving through. How does eleven work for you?"

"Just fine. I'll see you there."

Samantha replaced her phone in its cradle and poured the orange juice into a tall glass. She had yet to cover her cereal in milk, which was a good thing or it would have been a bit soggy by now. Taking the glass of juice and bowl of cereal to the table by the bay window, she sat down for breakfast. The sun was partially blocked by a large, white fluffy cloud, keeping its strength through the kitchen window at bay while she ate. Sometimes the sun was so powerfully strong coming through that window, she had to partially close the blinds, which she hated doing because her view was one she never tired of. She knew it wouldn't be long before the sun would be lower in the sky and the trees would start turning. With its changing of seasons, the varying degrees of light, and the intimate nature settings, there was always something for Samantha's camera to capture.

Jackson Hole was not a town for the weak. It took a level of durability to sustain living there. The winters were long, the terrain rugged, and the likelihood of running into a bear or an elk was about the same as running into another human. Even so, it attracted tourists passing through to experience the Grand Tetons, Jenny Lake, and Jackson Hole itself. Every season brought a different type of tourist. Winter and spring guided the skiers to the snowy terrain, while summer and fall brought campers and foliage seekers. Samantha wondered if it was a place she could make home as a single woman with an independent career. She fell so in love with the area that she promised herself she would stay for a year, and if it worked out, she would make it her home. That was several years ago, and when she traveled for photo shoots, she was always happy to return home.

At eleven o'clock when she walked into Annie's, she spotted Don sitting in a booth in the corner. It wasn't all that busy since the breakfast people had fanned out and it wasn't quite lunchtime. Samantha nodded hello to Don and made her way to the booth.

"Good morning," he said as he stood to greet her. "Thank you for coming out to meet me."

"Of course, Don. Always great to see you." Samantha took her seat and in moments the waitress, Blanche, came by and asked if she wanted anything to drink. After ordering an iced tea, Samantha turned her attention back to Don, who was working on a cup of coffee. "So, what's on your mind, Don?"

"We go pretty far back, Samantha. You're my best customer, for obvious reasons. So, I wanted to run this idea by you first." Don paused and took another sip of coffee while Samantha waited. "You see, I'm no spring chicken anymore. The wife is pushing me to retire." Don and his wife Kay had lived in Jackson Hole longer than most anyone else Samantha knew. "She wants me to sell the shop so I can travel with her. You know, Hawaii and all those places retired couples go."

"Wow, I guess that makes sense. I just figured you'd always be there to frame my work, Don." Samantha felt a slight sense of panic set in. She knew that Don and Steve, his assistant, knew how she liked her mats cut and work framed. "What about Steve?" she asked.

"Steve wants to stay on. It's his security, you know. But, he's afraid a new owner would squeeze him out. Like if they already have someone they want working for them. Anyway, what brings me here with you is that...well, I want you to have the shop, Samantha." Don rested his near empty coffee mug on the table just as Blanche came over with Samantha's iced tea and a pot of coffee to refill his mug.

After Blanche walked away, Samantha said, "What do you mean by *have*, Don?"

"I mean we'd work out a deal where you wouldn't have to put any money up front to own it. We could work out something where I'd take partial profits on a sliding scale that would fade out in five years. There'd be plenty for you and you'd be the sole owner with your own creative license to do what you want with the place. The only thing I ask is that you keep Steve on."

"This is so sudden, Don. I need to think about it, and see if I could even work it in with my travel schedule. But my interest is definitely there, and your offer is very generous."

Samantha thought about all the ideas she had had for that shop over the years. Ways to improve it, make it brighter and more engaging to visitors. She loved Don and appreciated all he had done for her, including the several times he rushed jobs for special orders. Because of that, she held back from giving him critical feedback on the shop. It needed new paint, new framed images on the walls, and the front door itself needed a bright color to pop from the street view. She had always imagined red with a gold knocker, even though no one needed to knock. She imagined a gold frame painted around the knocker and a person's face painted on the door, peeping up through the frame and around the knocker. The ideas she had were endless; she just never spoke a word about them to Don in fear of unintentionally insulting him or hurting his feelings. Deep down she also knew that someone like him would be reluctant to change. *If it ain't broken, don't try to fix it* were the words she imagined rolled through Don's mind when it came to the frame shop. But now he was handing her the key and the freedom to make it her own.

"Do Kay and Steve know about this? About me, I mean?" she asked.

"Yes, they know we're meeting. Kay and I have talked about the details, of course. Steve knows I'm pushing to keep him there. If you want it, of course. He's very excited about the chance to work with you, and Kay thinks it's the best solution. She adores you and knows you'd make the shop special with your creative flare and understanding of the industry."

"That's sweet of her, and I would. Tell you what, let me think about it and make some phone calls. I'll get back to you by Friday. Does that sound reasonable?"

Don smiled and shook Samantha's hand from across the table. "Anything is better than a flat out *no* right now. Please think it over and call me if you have any questions—any at all."

"I will. My biggest decisions are about the lifestyle changes it would mean for me. It's a big commitment to staying in the area."

"You've been here for so long now. It's your home, Samantha. Everyone here loves you."

"I know. I've just been very single and free for so long. I guess commitment isn't my thing whether it's in business or relationships. But this is quite an offer, and I already have some ideas, so let me get to them. I'll find you at the shop on Friday. Deal?"

"Deal," said Don.

Samantha took the last sip of iced tea, said goodbye to Don, and made her way back outside. The air was dry and warm and as she climbed in her Chevy Tahoe. She couldn't ignore the butterflies in her stomach and the level of excitement she felt when she thought about the frame shop being hers. It was simply named Jackson Hole Frame Shop, and it had a great reputation dating back to the sixties when Don first opened it. It had been the town's General Store until then. Over the years, a fair amount of tourists brought their printed images back on their next trips through town to have them framed by Don, and eventually Steve when he came on board. They knew that Don had a knack for it and had taught Steve all of his tricks of the trade. Samantha had little interest in doing any of the framing herself. If she had wanted to learn framing, she would have done so a while ago and probably would have saved herself more money than she would be willing to admit. But, she never had the desire. She preferred to be out capturing images and letting the professionals handle the mat cutting, framing, and especially handling the glass. If she took over the shop, she would most certainly count on Steve to carry that load while she worked on the rest.

Even with all of that, as Samantha backed out of her parking spot, she felt a surge of fear about giving up the freedom she was accustomed to. The fear engulfed her as equally as the entrepreneurial excitement of being a shop owner did. In the next five days, she would have to figure out a way to create a balance between the two in order to make it work, if that's what she decided she wanted. And it was determining that balance that would keep her awake at night.

*****

"You could stay here. I'd just need you in the shop while I'm traveling. You wouldn't have to see much of me, if that makes you feel better about it." Samantha bit down on her bottom lip to keep herself from saying much more. "You're the only one I know who can do this."

The silence on the other end of the phone lasted as long as Samantha would expect it to. Robert didn't make rash decisions, except for the one he made when he left her eight years earlier. They hadn't been together long, and the reality was, they grew to know each other better over the eight years since breaking up. Once the initial shock wore off, Samantha had found a place inside here where she was able to accept the ending of a relationship and the beginning of a friendship. It took a while, but in the process of it all, it managed to work itself into a friendship that they both valued. Both had dated others over the years, but neither married. If Robert hadn't been single right now, Samantha wouldn't have even asked him to cover for her at the shop. They often ran into problems where their relationship wasn't always accepted by a new partner. With all the explaining it took, they decided it was better to just not be in touch as much when the other was dating someone new.

Samantha could just about hear him thinking on the other end of the line, but was having a hard time gauging what his response would be. It was a lot to ask, especially because the favor—even though he would be paid—was dependent on her travel schedule. One of the qualities they had in common was their intense desire for independence.

"Okay, let's try it for six months then reevaluate where we are then," he finally said.

"You're kidding? You want to do this?"

"I just said I would. For six months, though. That's all I can commit to for now, so if you're going on some photo shoots, you better book them soon," Robert said. "Send me a letter of agreement that spells out the details."

"Certainly. I was thinking hourly plus I'd fly you here. You know I don't cook, but there'd be plenty of food and your favorite beer in the fridge. Just let me know ahead of time what you want in the fridge and I'll pick it up. This could work. Thank you!" Samantha was grinning into the phone, wishing he was there to hug, but then put away that thought. Their sexual attraction had remained as strong as their friendship, which was one reason they didn't see much of each other and why they backed off while dating someone else.

"Any idea when the transfer will take place? I'm sure you have a good attorney, but do you need me to read the contract over?" Robert had a strong business mind, which was one of the reasons why Samantha immediately thought of him. She knew that during the days or weeks he was at the shop, he would analyze the business side and ensure it was running efficiently. She, on the other hand, was a creative through and through. Though she'd hire an accountant or bookkeeper to handle the financials, she would value Robert's input just as much.

That Friday morning, Samantha walked into the Jackson Hole Frame Shop.

"Don? Are you here?" After no immediate answer, she worked her way to the back where she found Don organizing materials that had just come in. "There you are," she said.

"Samantha! I was hoping to see you this morning. Come in...please. Can I get you something to drink?"

"Oh, no, that's okay. I won't be too long," Samantha said as she put her purse down on a shelf next to her. She noticed the look on Don's face drop from optimism to worry with her last words. She was quick to allay is fear by saying, "I have a photo shoot on Jenny Lake I need to get to, but I wanted to stop by and let you know..." she paused for effect as Don froze, waiting for her response. When she smiled big, he smiled back, and she said, "You have yourself a deal!"

Don clapped his hands together, looked up to the ceiling, and then reached out to shake Samantha's hand. She leaned in and gave him a hug.

"God bless you for saying yes!" Don said as he embraced her like he would a daughter.

"What's all the commotion back here?" Steve asked as he walked in the backroom.

"Steve, my friend, you've got yourself a new boss!" said Samantha as she looked back and forth between the two men. Steve ran over and started to shake her hand, but she pulled him in for a hug, too. "We're all family. I don't break up families," she said. "Besides, other than Don himself, you're the best framer I know."

"Oh wow, thank you so much. You have no idea how much this means to me." Steve was beaming, shifting back and forth between his two feet.

"When can you meet to go over the contract?" Don asked. "Kay said she can cook a nice dinner and have you over to work it all out. That was if you said *yes*, of course! She'll be tickled pink hearing the news. I'm going to call her and set it up. How does Sunday work for you?"

"Sunday is just fine, Don." Samantha was grinning ear to ear, pleased to see the joy on Don's face and relief on Steve's.

"Great. Six o'clock. I'll have her cook something real good. You just bring your mind and pen!"

"You've got it," Samantha said. "And, Steve, I'll see you soon. We can discuss details next week. I have some ideas to run by you."

"Yes, ma'am. I'll be here."

Later that night Samantha was in her office organizing items that she would want to bring to the shop. She had a pile on one side of her desk that would go with her, and as she reached behind the desk to unplug her electric pencil sharpener, her shoulder bumped up against something. A split second later, she heard a crashing noise behind her. Startled, she looked down at the floor only to find the shattered glass from the frame holding the image of the construction workers.

"Crap!" Horrified at the sight before her, Samantha's heart sunk. Her muse was shattered into dozens of pieces. She looked down at the four construction worker faces smiling back up at her and bent down to pick up the larger pieces of glass to toss in the garbage can. She then gently placed the frame and print on her desk before going to find her vacuum to pick up the remaining shards of glass.

"I guess I've got a job for Steve," she said under her breath as she finished and silenced the roar of the Hoover. It was then when the phone rang.

"Hello?"

"Samantha? It's me," said Robert. "I heard your message. Congratulations!"

"Thanks. I'm nervous, but more excited than anything," she said as she put the vacuum back in the closet. "I'm going over Sunday night to iron out the details."

"Sounds great. Again, feel free to fax the contract over if you want me to look at it."

"I will. I'm sure it'll be fair and good, though. Don's a good guy."

"Okay, but still. I've gotta run, but we'll catch up when you're ready," said Robert.

Samantha hung up the phone and went back in the office. Carefully, she pulled the print from the remains of the wooden frame. Hanging it over the garbage can, she dangled it so any last bits of glass would fall into the can. In the bottom drawer of her desk were a handful of manila envelopes. She pulled one out and slid the photo inside.

*****

As she left Don and Kay's house, Samantha clung to a contract for the frame shop. She was more than satisfied with his offer and felt ready to embrace this new beginning, even if it meant taming her wandering soul a bit. Had it not been for Robert agreeing to help out, she would not have gone through with it.

Only a week later, after the contracts had been signed, Don handed Samantha the key to the shop in a rather unceremonious event at the diner. That was how both of them wanted it. The transition would be relatively easy since Steve was in the know of the day-to-day goings on. She sat down with him on the first day, a quiet morning, and went over all of her plans for upgrades and improvements. He nodded his head in agreement on each item and shared his excitement to help her out.

"Bring the paint, and I'll be ready!" said Steve. "I can't believe how great this is all going to be."

Samantha reached into her oversized bag and pulled out a manila envelope. "I just have one favor to ask." Samantha pulled out the image of the New York City construction workers.

"Sure, anything you need," said Steve.

"I need to have this image reframed. The frame broke the other night. It's my favorite photo." She placed the photo on the table between them.

"That's a great shot!" Steve said as he watched how Samantha handled it with the utmost care. "Let's look at some mats and frames for it." He gently took the photo from her as they walked over to the supplies in the workroom.

"I'll let you pick them. You'd know better than me," said Samantha. "I can take the photos, but this is your end. Just show me what you pick."

While Steve went through mats and frames, Samantha went to the front of the shop where Casper, the town's most eccentric artist, was working his way through the aisles in the shop.

"Good morning, can I help you, Casper?" asked Samantha.

"Hi there, Samantha. I heard you were taking over. Great to hear it," Casper tilted his head and tipped his hat at her. "I'm just picking up a few brushes. Working on something new."

"Perfect. Just let me know when you're ready."

Samantha looked through the two drawers next to the cash register, finding pens, pads of paper, batteries, a hammer, and other assorted odd-ball items. When Casper approached the register, he held three artists brushes in his hand. Samantha rang him up, and gave him thirty seven cents change from his bills. He smiled as he left, and Samantha listened as the bell above the door rang when he walked out onto the sidewalk.

While Samantha sorted through the wrinkled up bills, she noticed a one dollar bill with the name JACK SAMPSON written on the back.

"Jack Sampson?" she whispered to herself. "It couldn't be? Could it?"

Samantha's mind went back to a day and time when time wasn't tracked. It was the summer of 1984 between their high school graduation and going off to college. Jack and Samantha spent the summer swinging from a rope on a tree and dropping into the cold, flowing river. When they weren't wrapped up in a meal at the diner his mother worked at, they were wrapped up in one another's arms on his back porch. His mother worked till late at night, leaving Jack and Samantha with plenty of alone time. It was that fall when he left for college on the West Coast and she left for New York City. She never shared it with anyone, or even framed it for that matter, but her other favorite photo was one of Jack swinging on the tire swing just before dropping into the river. She had been standing on the riverbank and he was smiling big at her as he splashed into the water.

Samantha looked at the date on the bill. "Nineteen seventy-six? This bill has been around a lot longer than most one dollar bills would ever survive." She spoke aloud to no one but herself.

Samantha couldn't have known that the one dollar bill had been taped inside Jack's desk for nearly a decade. Nor could she know that it also sat in Carrie's dresser drawer until she saved enough money to buy her new pair of Pumas. The one dollar bill had indeed been preserved.

Samantha tucked the bill in her shirt pocket and called to Steve, "I'll be right back. You okay by yourself?"

"Yes, go right ahead," Steve called to her. "Just finding the right colors for your photo here."

"Don't start framing it yet. I have something I need to put in it."

"Gotcha!"

Samantha climbed in her SUV and drove the few miles to her house. She kept the one dollar bill on the seat next to her, looking down at it every once in a while. She hadn't seen Jack in years, and now here was his one dollar bill on the seat next to her.

Back in her home office, Samantha pulled a shoebox out of her closet. The box was stored in there when she first moved to Jackson Hole, but she still knew by heart every item it held. When she removed the lid, there in the midst of the materials was the photo of Jack on the tire swing. She held it up and looked at it under the light by the window. A smile slowly came to her as the memories flooded back.

"Oh Jack, you were a good soul," she whispered. From her pocket she pulled out the dollar bill. Even though Jack's name was written in all capital letters, they were enough that she could compare them to the writing on the envelopes and in the letters he sent to her from college. The stack was to one side of the shoebox, tied with a long, red ribbon. She peeled the ribbon off the end of the batch. Her address in New York City and his in California covered the front of the envelopes. Though he would have only been ten when he wrote his name on that bill, she knew it was indeed the handwriting of the Jack Sampson she had loved, and still had love for. Her feelings for him hadn't changed all that much in the ten years since they dated and wrote each other transcontinental love letters that would eventually fade as they moved on with their lives. She had suppressed her feelings for him so she could focus on her career, and yet she kept the memories and emotions stored in a section of her heart that could never break. He had been the love of her life; she only saw that in hindsight when life went on and love never showed itself in the same way. Robert certainly hadn't begun to cast a similar light in her life.

Samantha coupled the one dollar bill with the photo, placed them in her shirt pocket, and made her way back to the frame shop.

"Steve, before you put the paper on the back, I want to tuck these two items in the frame. Could you tape them side by side to the back of the photo so they'll stay behind the paper?"

Steve looked at her quizzically, but didn't verbally question his new boss. "Yes, ma'am. Whatever you want." He didn't ask who Jack Sampson was or who the young man on the tire swing in the photo was. Nor did he question what either had to do with a photo of construction workers. Some stories were private, and he respected that. If he had asked questions of every photo he framed, he'd have a book to write.

Two days later, Samantha opened the shop at ten a.m. and on the desk in the office was the framed photo of the construction workers and a note from Steve saying, "They're behind the paper backing, taped to the back of the photo...just like you asked."

Samantha smiled and hung the photo above her new desk in her new office.

Jack

2000

"Mr. Sampson, line two is for you."

"Thank you, Sarah." Jack picked up his phone, holding it in his palm for a moment. He knew who was on the other end of the line without having to ask. Sarah was used to him not asking who was calling. She learned a while ago that he liked the challenge of guessing who it was, and she liked that he was usually right. This time he didn't have to guess. The call was expected to come in at eleven o'clock a.m., and though it was four minutes past the hour, he didn't judge the four minutes he'd been tapping his pen on his desk. He did, however, judge the seconds, because they seemed to last much longer.

"Hello, this is Jack," he said after pushing the flashing button for line two.

"Mr. Sampson, this is Doctor Williams over at Stanford Hospital."

"Yes, Doctor Williams, I've been expecting your call. How is she?" Jack spun his chair around to look out over the Embarcadero and the Bay Bridge. From sixteen floors up, it was an impressive view, even on a foggy day when only the tips of the bridge were visible. Eleven years had passed since the 1989 Loma Prieta earthquake. Jack took the job at Golden Gate Publications in San Francisco just months before at the young age of twenty-three. Breaking news about the earthquake during the Bay Bridge Series created long hours at the office. Monthly magazine issues are typically planned at least three months in advance of their release, but in the situations of breaking news, it took long hours to rearrange layout and pen articles in time for the next possible release. Weeklies and newspapers had it easier, but monthly magazines suffered under pressure. But, the cover turned out to be the most compelling of all, the articles heart-warming, and in the end Golden Gate Publications won an award for its coverage.

Naturally, Jack didn't have the prime corner office then. He started out fresh out of college as an intern writing copy and editing articles. But, he worked his way up. In fact, he worked his way so far up he bought out the owner when he retired seven years after Jack started. It was Jack's thirtieth birthday present to himself, he told his friends. But, the company was thriving and there was really no thought needed about deciding to buy it, only negotiations, which were handled by a team of lawyers. The papers were signed and when Mr. Tanner retired, a big dinner in his honor was planned and enjoyed at the San Francisco Yacht Club. At the end of the evening, a toast was made and Mr. Tanner handed over a golden pen to Jack.

Sylvia had been there. Jack flew her in for the event. Though she told him she felt completely out of place in a large city, let alone at a prestigious yacht club, she was too proud of him not to come. It had been her first time flying. The second was when she was diagnosed with Eisenmenger Syndrome.

"Jack, I'm sorry to say that your mother's condition is worse than I first expected."

Jack took a deep breath and waited for the next sentence.

"Let me explain what's going on and then you can decide how you and Sylvia want to proceed. Eisenmenger's syndrome is really a combination of two problems. Your mother has a hole between two of her cardiac chambers. This allows the oxygenated blood to recirculate back into the right ventricle, which then goes to the lungs instead of flowing out of the left ventricle to the rest of the body. Does that make sense?"

"Yes," Jack said. "Keep going. I'm listening."

"If enough time has passed before this is caught, the extra blood flow to her lungs will damage the vessels, which will cause high pressures or pulmonary hypertension. This, if you can picture it, reverses the flow of blood, so the deoxygenated, instead of the oxygenated blood, flows out to the rest of the body."

"I understand," Jack said with a sigh he tried to stifle.

"The second problem is the result of all of that. It creates cyanosis, or simply known as low oxygen content, in the blood." Doctor Williams paused before delivering the next bit of news. "Eventually, Jack, this causes failure of the right ventricle. Your mother's right ventricle is quite damaged. More so than I thought."

"So, what are our options?" Jack spun his chair back around to his desk and took the golden pen from its place under a lamp. He held it over a pad of paper ready to write whatever Doctor Williams would say next because Jack knew he'd have to see it on paper in order to wrap his head around it.

"Well, in younger patients, when we do the echocardiogram that we just did on your mother, it not only tells us where the defect is, but it measures the pressure in the right ventricle and the lungs. We can then do a heart catheterization, a relatively simple procedure where a catheter is threaded through the blood vessels into the heart. This procedure tells us the size of the hole and measures pressure within the heart. In young kids, we can usually resolve the issue because their arteries can handle the invasion of the catheter. In your mother's case, her right ventricle is so damaged that I'm concerned the catheterization could cause more problems. We have a team of experts here, of course, and we would do all we could do. It's really up to you and Sylvia if you want her to have the catheterization."

71

Jack put the pen down without writing a word. He had heard enough to know that he had to go to the hospital and talk to his mother.

"Thank you, Doctor Williams. I have faith in your team if we decide to go that route. I need to come over to see my mother."

"I understand. You have my number, of course. Call me when you've made a decision or if you have any questions."

"Doc, what if she doesn't do it? Then what?" Jack asked, not really wanting to hear the answer he knew was coming.

"Well, it would be a matter of time, Jack. We would keep her quite comfortable. Sadly, right ventricular dysfunction is the strongest predictor of a negative outcome. I know this isn't an easy decision, so take your time. We're taking good care of her."

"Would you say it's a matter of months? Her birthday is in April..."

"Jack, it's only February. I can't say for sure, but you have some time to think about your options. But, if it were me, I wouldn't take too long to decide if you're going to go through with the procedure. The damage can only get worse."

"Thank you. I'll call you."

Jack hung up the phone, grabbed his jacket from the hook on the back of the door, walked out of his office and told Sarah to take messages or let his calls go to voicemail. She nodded, knowing not to ask any questions.

After handing his car keys to the valet attendant, Jack made his way through the automatic doors to the hospital. The septic odor overwhelmed his nostrils as the doors flew open, pushing the inside air out. He didn't need to stop at the information desk; he knew where his mother's room was. She'd been there for five days already, undergoing more tests in those five days than he'd endured in his thirty-three years. Her arms were bruised from the blood sucking needles and a few *new on the job* phlebotomists.

His pace quickened as Jack made a turn at the next hallway. Sylvia's room was the fifth one down on the right. The irony of her room number being 630 didn't escape Jack. June thirtieth had been his father's birthday. Both he and his mother paused while reading her check-in papers when they saw the room number noted. They had glanced at one another, but didn't say anything. There was no need; each knew what the other was thinking.

Now, as Jack entered room 630, the only noise was the hum of the air conditioning under the windowsill and the soft snoring of his mother, tiny and frail under the sheet with a thin cotton blanket pulled up to her chin. Loose hair fell across her forehead, and her wrinkles were softened without any expression. Her laugh lines from the decades of pleasing customers at the diner now signified an old woman, even though she'd only just celebrated her fifty-second birthday.

Jack draped his jacket over the back of the chair in the corner. He went to the window and glanced outside to the view of the city below. The blinds were down all the way, but leveraged with the slats half opened. The noon sun was strong and he could feel the heat emanating off the glass.

"Jack, dear, is that you?" Sylvia's weak voice emerged from the bed. Jack turned to see his mother's face. It looked a bit paler since the day before, and a hint of blue seemed to cast across the shadows under her eyes and around her mouth.

"Hi, Mom. Yes, it's me. Are you comfortable?" Jack walked over to the side of the bed and instinctively pulled the thin white blanket up over his mother's shoulders. "How about something to drink...maybe some apple juice?"

Sylvia looked up at her only son and shook her head *no*. A tear began to form in the corner of her left eye. It never rolled down her cheek, but Jack watched it as it grew and rounded out before she wiped it away as if it were only a mere nuisance.

"What's wrong, Jack? You have a look...I know my boy." Sylvia forced a deep breath while she waited for Jack to answer.

With his left hand, Jack pulled a chair over and placed it next to his mother's bed. He sat down and looked at Sylvia. "We need to make a decision."

"What kind of decision, Jack? My will is already..."

"No, Mom, it's not that." Jack stopped her, not wanting to hear talk of a will. He knew she had nothing to leave him other than the house and some small items. He had been providing for her for years even though she refused to quit waitressing until recently.

"Then what? What is it?"

Not wanting to leave her worrying more than she had to, Jack presented her with the options the doctor gave him. Have the high risk procedure or live out her days in peace and quiet. Neither had a pleasant ending. Both made his stomach turn as he gave his mother the diluted details, leaving out the medical language, like the oxygenated and deoxygenated details.

"What do you think we should do? I can't decide this," said Sylvia. "I don't know what to say, Jack."

"Me neither, Mom. And you know what? We don't have to decide right now. Let's both sleep on it. Dr. Williams can answer any questions we have tomorrow." Jack stood and went to the

74

window, fighting back tears he didn't want his mother seeing. The sun was setting, leaving a glorious pink and red glow in the sky. "Can you see the sunset, Mom? See the colors?"

"Yes, Jack. I can see them from here."

"Let me prop your bed up a bit more," said Jack as he gathered his composure and made his way to the side of his mother's bed that had the buttons to adjust the bed's height. "There, is that better?"

"Yes, it's lovely out there...isn't it?" Sylvia's voice forced strength that Jack new was only for his benefit.

"Yes, it is."

"Remember how I'd bring you food home from the diner. Sal would load up a plate for you every night and send it home with me. He said to say hello and that he misses you around town. He knows you're a hot shot magazine publisher now. It makes him happy to know someone in that little town made something of themselves, but even happier that it was you."

Jack sat in the chair and listened as his mother talked.

"And did I tell you that Blake took over his pop's shop? Poor Graham. Heart attack under a car. Did you know that, Jack?"

"Yes, Momma. You told me so." Jack squeezed his mother's hand. "How 'bout the Cooper boys?"

"Oh those boys. The youngest grew up to be a fine boy, but those older ones, they're still trouble. I was glad when you were old enough that you didn't have to go there no more. Mrs. Cooper is a fine woman, but those boys, well they must've taken after their daddy. Never saw much of him. Heard he ran off with that teacher...what was her name?"

"Ms. Carlson, I bet."

"Oh yes, that's her. Tramp. Poor Mrs. Cooper, but she's probably better off anyways..." Sylvia's words trailed off, lingering in the thick air of the hospital room.

That night Jack slept in the chair next to her bed. Both he and Sylvia slept until the nurse's two a.m. vitals check.

Samantha

2000

Jackson Hole's only quiet season seemed to be early spring when the snow melted into mud and the flowers had yet to bloom. Samantha had already hosed down the mat at the front door of the shop twice that week, freeing it of the clumps of mud that stuck to it like gum in a child's hair.

"Your exhibit photos are done, Samantha," said Steve. "I laid them out on the work table for you to see."

Samantha's next exhibit was at the Fog and Sand Gallery in San Francisco in three weeks, which was the first week in May. The selected, framed eight images were due to ship to them by Wednesday, and seeing that it was Monday, she was under a tight deadline to send them out the door. She would ask Steve if he would help pack them, as the shop often provided that service for clients who left images to be framed, asking to have them shipped to their homes around the world when they were ready. Steve had become a master at packing frames, large and small, just right.

"Well, let's go take a look!" said Samantha as she closed the cash register drawer. She had been closing out the drawer for the night, about ready to make the bank deposit.

Back in the workroom she looked over her photos. Steve had done a remarkable job of selecting the appropriate mats that heightened the tones in each of the images. They were double matted and each one was framed in an elegant black frame for consistency. Samantha tended to avoid frames that distracted from the image. Too many times she saw framed work on display

77

and later could remember the frame, but not the subject of the photo. She preferred to choose a frame that enhanced the photo, one with a particular mat that worked with it as a complement to both the frame and image itself. Over the years, Steve had adapted that art to the point where she trusted his matting selection with almost every one of her projects, and even more so to the point where she rarely questioned his selections. There were times when she had a specific color combination in mind, but most of the time, she left it to his honed, professional eye.

As she looked over the current selection, she was as impressed as she'd ever been. "You really outdid yourself this time, Steve," she said, beaming.

"Maybe that's because of the subjects. I know them so well," said Steve.

Though Samantha had traveled the world in her decades of photography, this particular gallery fell in love with her Jackson Hole images. She eyed the Jenny Lake image from three fall seasons ago. The golden leaves reflecting in the lake was one of her favorites. But, it was the capture of the famous Mormon Row Moulton Barn that the Fog and Sand Gallery truly fell in love with, as had she. The famed barn was one that every photographer in the world who has passed through seemed to have captured. But, her version of the famed barn was extra special. It had an energy that everyone said they couldn't put a finger on; it was just different from the rest. It was almost as though the barn stood taller and prouder for her and her alone. The backstory as to why she captured it in the first place tied her to it emotionally. The day she took the photo, Robert had been in town visiting. They were sitting on the couch in the midst of one of their, "What do we do about us?" conversations. Though he had left her eight years earlier, their passion for one another never dwindled. The conversation during that visit grew to the point where the words were becoming heated, which usually meant an equally heated romp in the bedroom when they were done. But, this time she stopped it before it went there.

"I'm going for a drive. I'll be back," she said, leaving Robert stunned and silent since she had never broached their conversations that way. She picked her camera up off the kitchen counter, as it was never out of reach, and headed out in her Chevy Tahoe for a drive. It was that evening when the barn had an ethereal glow to it. The sun was setting and the snow-capped mountains, the barn's backdrop, catered to the light hitting their peaks and valleys. Each wooden board of the barn, each gap between them, and each frame of the doors and windows just about smiled back at her. She set up her tripod, set the aperture to 11.0, bracketing her exposure, and adjusted the shutter speed to accommodate. When it all came together in the darkroom late that night, she knew it would be a gallery show-stopper. That night Samantha learned a valuable lesson; that walking away from a heated discussion was okay. And that nothing could squelch her muse—it was *always* alive within her.

Robert was asleep when she got home and didn't hear her in the darkroom. The next morning he cooked her breakfast and the conversation about their relationship was shelved. Other than having their makeup sex, they tiptoed around one another until Robert left two days later. That was not only the last time they slept together, but it was also the last time they had seen one another. The fact that he was coming back into town to cover the shop while she was at the exhibit reception in three weeks hadn't been far from her mind. In the time since she'd taken over the frame shop, he had yet to have to help out. Their initial agreement was six months, and that quickly came and went without her needing him. She had been too busy acquainting herself with the shop and making the changes she wanted to make. Don approved of all of her changes except that she replaced the coffee maker with a new one. He insisted the old one was good luck, and she insisted it made the worst coffee she'd ever tasted. He had just come back from his and Kay's first trip to Hawaii as retirees and that, of course, was the first thing he noticed.

"Hey, it's your shop now. But, I'm just telling you, that coffee maker was good luck." He was so serious that Samantha felt guilty, but when she went to pour her next cup of coffee, the guilt waned and she went out and bought a new one. Don's sat in the same place next to the new one that made perfect coffee every time.

"How do you like them?" asked Steve.

"They're perfect! Thank you." Samantha hesitated, not sure how to ask him if he could package them up, but Steve read her mind.

"Great, I'll get these all boxed up for you. Just give me the address of the gallery for the label and anything else you might need to include."

"You're the best."

Samantha fetched the address for him then went back to her office and sat at her desk to pour through orders she needed to place. Surprisingly, she had grown more accustomed to committing time to the shop than she anticipated. She found time in the early morning and late evenings to spend capturing photos, which were ideal hours anyway. The combination created a balance and quality of life she was growing to enjoy. Her share of traveling would come this month when she would fly to San Francisco for the gallery opening. It was an exhibit that featured six photographers, each of whom she looked forward to meeting. The reception was Thursday, May fourth, and she would stay in town for Cinco de Mayo celebrations. She looked forward to being amidst the crowded streets and the noises that only a city could evoke. Living in Jackson Hole meant the howl of a wolf under the moon and stars, not the sound of a bus taking off en route to its next stop or the echo of bands playing in bars on the corner or the chatter and laughter in crowds enjoying a rare warm day in Golden Gate Park.

The ringing of the phone interrupted her note taking for the next order.

"Jackson Hole Frame Shop," she said as she held the phone between her cheek and shoulder so she could continue typing.

"Hi Samantha, it's me."

She stopped typing when she heard Robert's voice. "Hello there. Are you ready to come out next month?" she asked.

"Yes, just checking flights now. Tell me again when you're leaving?"

"I fly out on May fourth—early in the morning. So maybe you could come on the second or third. I can show you around the shop before I go." Samantha gathered that he felt the same way about not wanting to spend too many nights together before she left. At the same time, she needed to give him the tour of the shop; even though Steve would be able to do it, she really wanted to.

"I have a meeting on the second, but could fly out early on the third," he said.

"Great. If you're here by lunchtime, we'd have plenty of time."

"Are you excited for the exhibit?" he asked.

"Yes, and about being in San Francisco. I'm going to take advantage of the photo opportunities while I'm there, of course. I rented a car so I can go up into the Marin Headlands or down to Half Moon Bay. Maybe both if I can work it right," she said. She had already planned specific bluffs she wanted to capture during the golden and blue hours of sunset and sunrise.

"Well, make sure you have warm clothes. You know that Mark Twain once said that the coldest winter he ever spent was a summer in San Francisco," said Robert.

"Oh, I know. The fog will be good to photograph though," she said. "We don't get too much of it here."

"Always about what's on the other end of the lens, isn't it?" Robert chuckled. "Okay, I'll go book the ticket. I'll plan to leave on Monday morning since you get back late Sunday night."

"Sounds good. And, thank you!"

Samantha went back to filling out the order, ensuring that the shop would be stocked well while Robert was in town. When she finished, she called to Steve, "I'm running to the bank and the diner. Can I get you anything while I'm out?"

After hearing a *no*, Samantha picked up her purse and walked out onto the streets of Jackson Hole. The town was small and rustic, not quaint like a coastal town might be. It carried a masculine energy that she enjoyed and felt safe in. She knew that Don was right; it was unlikely that she'd ever leave. She had made it her home after a few years of living in New York City and traveling around the globe on photo shoots. After only a few months of being there, she felt like she had finally found her real home. It came at a time when she needed that—a place to ground her flight-tempted wings, but also know that she could fly away on assignment when she wanted. It wasn't like when she lived in New York, a place where everyone fit in. New Yorkers felt like they were one of many. In Jackson Hole, she felt it was uniquely hers even though she shared it with others. It was theirs, too, but in their own personal way. For Samantha, the way her camera captured the nooks and crannies of the surrounding landscape made it a more intimate setting for her. She knew its light, its seasons, its temperament, and its climate. She was intimate with it in ways no one else could be any more than she would understand their connection to it. To fully embrace a life with it, you had to accept all of it. There was no way around it. It was that kind of place.

The opening of the front door to the diner created a jingle from the bell strapped to the top of the door frame. Blanche hollered a hello from across the room and signaled that she'd be right over. Samantha took a seat in the booth in the corner, picking up a left behind newspaper off the counter.

"What can I get you, Samantha?" Blanche asked as she approached. She pulled her pen from behind her ear and prepared to write, even though Samantha often ordered the same lunch.

Samantha didn't even have to open a menu. "My usual. Grilled cheese on wheat with provolone and tomato. Side of fries would be great, and an iced tea." She craved comfort food when she was stressed, and the idea of seeing Robert in a few weeks was stressing her more than she was admitting to herself. The intensity of feelings would amplify, like it always did, in the days leading up to his arrival. She was already thinking of the dozens of ways they could keep busy, and hence keep them out of the bedroom. The shop would serve as the main distraction, and luckily she would be leaving the next day.

While eating lunch, Samantha took out a notepad and began writing down notes for her trip to San Francisco. She hadn't been in years and was anxious to visit again, not only for the gallery reception, but as she told Robert, for the unlimited photo opportunities. Her long weekend would be packed between the gallery reception and exhibit followed by photo shoots that meant anticipating lighting and running from one spot to another with her camera and gear. She wondered how much worse traffic would be nowadays, compared to her last visit there, and made a note to inquire with Fog and Sand. They would know. She also jotted down all of the gear and accessories she wanted to take along. She was never one to travel light; it was virtually impossible if she wanted to be prepared for any situation from lighting to climate, and it had always been worth the effort. Except for one time when she left her heavier tripod behind on a trip, settling for the lighter weighted one. Between the winds and lack of stability during certain shots, she regretted not having the more durable, sturdy one beneath her camera. The slightest bit of camera shake isn't noticeable on smaller prints, but becomes rather obvious when enlargements are printed. She found a workaround on that trip, but ever since then, she made no excuses about bringing the best gear for the job.

"Need anything else?" Blanche asked. Samantha hadn't noticed her approaching the table.

"Just the bill, Blanche. Thank you," said Samantha. She put her pen back in her purse and pulled out her wallet. When Blanche returned with the bill, Samantha left enough cash on the table for her lunch and a tip.

"Thank you! See you next time," Samantha said as she walked out the door. The early spring air and midday sun felt good on her face as she walked over to her Tahoe and climbed in. She had one more stop to make before going back to the shop and relieving Steve for his own lunch break.

There were no department stores in Jackson Hole, something Samantha had to adjust to after living in New York City where Jimmy Choo and Bergdorf Goodman were at her feet. When she left New York, she chose to leave that wardrobe behind as well. For one thing, she would have stood out as a tourist in a town she was making her home. Designer skirts and dresses turned into jeans and flannel shirts or shorts and tank tops, key wardrobe elements for any Grand Teton or Yellowstone photo shoot. But, with Robert coming to town, she wanted to find some nice lingerie. Her mind battled with itself, knowing she wanted to resist him, but also knowing there would be no way she could. The latter always won.

She found relief when she entered a quiet shop. Surely running into locals while buying sexy lingerie would raise eyebrows. Rumors would whirl about town like tumbleweed— impossible to catch and ever growing. The owner was a sweet older woman who had no shame when it came to the importance of just the right lingerie to "set the mood," as she liked to call it. The last time Samantha had been in there was the last time Robert came to town, but the woman remembered her. Samantha tended to stand out from the locals despite her efforts to fit in. She was tall and lean with a million dollar smile that stopped men in their tracks. She tended to hide behind her camera to downplay her outward beauty, but it didn't work as she expected it to. In fact, it likely enhanced it. She often caught a glimpse of wives elbowing their husbands after passing her by on the street. But, it was that same smile that patrons to the frame shop were drawn to.

"May I help you?" The elderly woman came out from behind a sales rack.

"I'll browse, but will certainly ask if I have questions," Samantha responded. To her, lingerie was such a personal choice that she didn't want the help. She also knew what Robert liked.

Within minutes of browsing, her eye caught a lace-lined, black corset. Long ribbons wove through eyelets on the back, tying at the bottom with extra to spare for any necessary adjustments. She pulled it off the rack and held it out in front of her. From previous purchases, she knew it would fit. She also knew it would look fabulous and that it would drive Robert crazy.

"I'll take this," she said. Five minutes later, she left the shop with the corset neatly wrapped in a box, tucked in a bag.

When she walked back in the frame shop, Steve said, "Everything is packed and ready to ship."

"Terrific. Thank you!" Samantha instinctively walked over and inspected the packages. True to Steve's packaging talents, the framed items were tightly packed and ready to go.

"Is UPS Second Day Air okay?" asked Steve.

"That would be perfect. They'll have it on Thursday, which gives them several days to hang them."

"Are you getting nervous? About the opening?"

"A little. It's always exciting and nerve racking at the same time. You never know how many people will show up. This is a good gallery in a great district, so we'll see!"

Samantha closed the desk drawer and Steve nodded at her and excused himself to stack the packages closer to the door. He had packed each and every framed image with extra care and would be relieved when they reached the gallery without incident.

Back in her office, Samantha sat back in her chair and twirled her hair with her right hand. She did that when she was deep in thought, and this time her thoughts were on Robert's arrival the next week. Their agreement for him to come to help out with the frame shop while she was gone stood, but she wasn't sure she could keep the agreement she made to herself to not sleep with him. That was already evident by the errand she ran.

Jack

2000

Two days had passed since Jack spoke to Doctor Williams, and he knew that if they didn't make a decision, it would be made for them. He felt trapped between door one and door two, neither of which had the promising outlook he had hoped for when he first brought Sylvia out to Stanford. Sal had called Jack from the diner on a Sunday evening when Sylvia wasn't working. He described the differences he'd seen in Sylvia over the past few months and shared his concerns. Sylvia was too proud, and even a little too stubborn, to seek medical attention on her own, and Sal knew he had to alert Jack.

"She seems, I don't know, maybe winded, even just carrying a handful of plates to the kitchen. She's family to us, Jack, you know that. But, she's your mother and she loves you very much. I know she'd be better off coming out to you where you can get her to the best doctors," Sal had said.

"Thank you, Sal. I appreciate you calling me. Say hello to your wife for me."

Jack hung up from that call and dialed his travel agent, who made arrangements to fly Sylvia out on Wednesday. Once settled, he called Sylvia and gave her no choice in the matter. She didn't fight him on it, mostly because she wanted to see her son and partly because she knew she needed the care of a doctor, and that Jack would only send her to the best.

Initially the hospital intimidated both of them, but now that she had been there for nearly a week, it was starting to feel normal, something Jack never anticipated from a hospital. He knew all the nurses and even a few orderlies. Creating a balance between work and tending to his mother was a bit of a struggle, but his staff picked up the slack and he would reward them accordingly.

Jack sat at his desk with his head planted in the palms of his hands. He rubbed at his left temple to try to eradicate the headache that hadn't gone away in several hours. The bottle of cold water he bought on the way to the office was now lukewarm and untouched. The bit of the bottle's condensation had long since dried, but his eyes were another thing. They welled up with tears of frustration, confusion, and indecision. How was he supposed to choose which route to take for his mother's care? He was not a doctor. *They are the professionals and should know better. How is it possible this became his choice?*

Jack reached over and picked up the phone. As he dialed the now familiar number, he waited for Doctor Williams to answer, but when the voicemail kicked in, all he could do was slam the phone back down.

"Is everything okay?" Sarah asked as she cracked the door open. A look of compassion filled her face. Jack felt awkward having her see him this way, and waved his emotions away, dismissively at the air.

"Yeah, just can't get through to the doctor. I'm going over to the hospital." Jack stood and pulled his jacket from the back of his chair. "I'll check in later," he said as he tried not to brush too abruptly past Sarah, who had stepped, nearly tiptoeing, back into the hallway.

After he hit the button for the elevator, Jack ran back for the water bottle off his desk. He knew it would help his headache. The elevator door opened just as he returned. He opened the bottle and took a long drink as the elevator lowered itself to the lobby. Once outside, the cool air felt good on his face as he walked down the street. He'd eventually grab a cab over to the hospital, but he needed to walk a few blocks first.

The fluorescent lights in the hallway at the hospital flickered as Jack paced up and down them. The nurse said that Sylvia had fallen asleep a few hours after eating a snack of applesauce. She was holding steady, for now. Jack asked them to page Dr. Williams, and within ten minutes, the nurse called him to the phone.

"Dr. Williams?"

"Yes, Jack."

"I'm...well, I honestly just don't know what to do. Neither of the choices seem fair or right. And yet, if I don't choose, I lose her anyway."

"Jack, she's losing strength, so if we do the procedure, we should do it tomorrow. Otherwise, well, we've discussed it already, but if you..."

"No, I know. I know you're doing all you can given her health. I think we should do the procedure. I don't want to wish later that we didn't try, and this state of limbo isn't helping." Jack looked down the hall to the room his mother slept in. He felt bad making the decision for her, but she had given him power of attorney and he felt it was the right thing to do.

"Okay, then. We will do this in the morning. Be at the hospital by six o'clock," said Dr. Williams.

"I will."

Jack put the phone down and turned away from the nurses' station before they could see the tears welling up. He walked down the hall, hugging closely to the wall, until he reached Sylvia's room. The door was slightly ajar, but the lights were out. The blinds were closed and the only light came from the cardiac machines. The indications of life; her heart rate and oxygen levels flashed as the EKG lines scrolled across the screen. As he stepped closer, he could hear her breath as she slept rolled on her side and facing the window. Jack pulled the chair over to her bed and sat down. He took his own deep breath and slowly let it out.

On Sylvia's left hand was the gold wedding band Greg had put on her finger all those years ago. It stayed on her finger, letting the men know she was taken. Finding another man never crossed her mind. Greg had been the love of her life since they first met in English class in eighth grade. He was new to the school after his family moved to town from North Dakota. The first day of school, he sat behind her and yanked on her long ponytail. She turned around, ready to give him a piece of her mind, but the moment she glimpsed his hazel eyes, she was smitten and the only words that came out of her mouth were, "New are you? I'm Sylvia." He walked her home after school and they married seven years later. When Jack was born, Sylvia didn't want another child. She was happy with one child, and Greg was happy when she was happy. Jack's birth had been relatively easy, likely due to Sylvia's wide hips and partly because he was only six pounds and seven ounces. The first look at his cheeks and tiny fingers filled a space in her heart that she hadn't known craved that kind of love.

Greg looked at both Jack and Sylvia as miracles. He worked hard every day to keep his family happy, food on the table, and the roof over their heads. His life insurance policy had paid off the house, and Sylvia never left. The walls were filled with memories from their few years together in it, and she wasn't about to abandon those walls. The thought of another family's laughter and cheer echoing in the hallways was too painful to imagine. So, she kept working for Sal and living in the house.

Greg's death shocked Sylvia and the community. Jack was too young to understand when the Illinois State Trooper came to the door late on a Tuesday night. The rain poured down, running off the rim of the trooper's hat, as he stood at the door. Sylvia shook as she invited him in. Jack sat on the stairs, but all he remembers from that night was how the flashing red and blue lights came through the living room window and reflected off the trooper's badge. That, and how his mother sunk into his arms after he spoke the words, "I'm sorry..." Jack wondered why his mother was hugging the trooper, and even more so, why she was crying so hard. After the trooper left, his father never came back. It took years for Jack to understand that night. He had suppressed it quite a bit until high school when he was watching a movie with Samantha, his girlfriend. There was a similar scene when a trooper came to the door of a family and announced the death of a husband to his wife. For years, Jack didn't recall the rest of the movie, only that scene. The scene put Jack in shock as the memories poured back into his conscious. The red and blue lights reflecting on the trooper's badge. His mother holding onto him for her own life. Jack sitting on the steps and watching the scene unfold.

"Are you okay?" Samantha had asked. Jack was visibly upset, to the point of trembling, during that scene. Samantha took his hand in hers and looked at him.

"No. Not really. That scene just reminded me of something."

Jack blinked back tears and squeezed Samantha's hand. They spent the rest of the night talking about the night Jack recalled finding out his father had died. Too young, too naïve, he could not have grasped the magnitude of the loss he and his mother would feel in very different ways.

This time there was no trooper. There was a doctor with a divided prognosis; one that forced Jack to choose the sharks in one pool of water versus the sharks in another pool. Different sharks, same danger, and the same outcome in the end.

"Jack, boy, come here," Sylvia said. Jack didn't mind that she still called him "boy." He thought it funny that parents often had nicknames for their children, but for the child, the parent was always mom or mother or dad or father or some kind of variance of "parent." *Why didn't nicknames work both ways?*

"I'm here. Can I get you something? Water or Ginger Ale?" Jack stood by the bed and took his mother's hand in his. She shook her head no.

"What does the doctor say?" Sylvia's voice was noticeably weaker than when she was first admitted to the hospital.

"They're doing to do a procedure tomorrow morning. Let's be hopeful that it helps you to feel better, okay?" Jack squeezed her hand gently as she blinked a yes at him.

"Get your rest for tomorrow," he told her. She closed her eyes and Jack sat back down in the chair, where he spent a sleepless night.

A nurse came through the door at not quite six the next morning. She took Sylvia's vitals and began prepping her for the procedure. Jack walked alongside the gurney as the orderly walked them down the hall to the elevator. Sylvia was too sleepy to talk, which was just as well. When they arrived at the operating room, Jack was instructed to wait in the waiting room and was told they would come find him when she was done. Jack kissed his mother on her head and whispered, "I love you. It will be fine. Everything is fine."

The doublewide doors swung open as Jack watched his mother being wheeled down the short hall to the sterile operating room. His last glimpse of her was as they turned into the operating room. He could make out her small frame under the blanket and her tuff of hair on the pillow. The doublewide doors closed at the same pace they opened, and when there was nothing left to see, Jack turned and started down the hall to a bench about halfway down. Unable to walk further at the moment, he sat on the bench and stared at the ceiling. *Please, God, take care of her. Please.*

Jack

2000

Doctor Williams didn't have to say anything to Jack when he walked toward him down the hall. Despair was written across his face.

"No!" Jack cried out before Doctor Williams could reach out and put a hand on his shoulder.

"We did everything we could, Jack. Sylvia was a fighter, but her heart, well...it wasn't a strong as she was. I'm so sorry."

Jack, still sitting, placed his face in his hands and for the first time since he lost his father, he cried like the same four year old boy. Doctor Williams sat down next to him and let Jack cry. He hadn't known Jack or Sylvia long, but their mother-son connection was stronger than most he had seen.

"You did all you could do." Jack started. "I knew the risks— I just couldn't prepare myself for the loss," Jack looked away from Doctor Williams and up at the ceiling in dismay. "I wasn't prepared for how it would feel."

"I know, Jack. No one is ever prepared for it, even when knowing the odds and likelihood. It doesn't change the loss felt when the time comes. Again, I am so sorry. I know how close you and Sylvia were. I admired that."

"Thanks," said Jack, choking back tears.

"I'll have the social worker contact you about the remaining details, okay?"

"Sure. Do that," said Jack. Looking around, but not finding a tissue, he tapped into that same four year old boy and wiped his face with his sleeve. *Sorry, mom. There just isn't a tissue around.*

When Jack stood to walk, his feet were heavy—his heart even more so. Though he was certain they had seen plenty of grown men cry, he avoided eye contact when he passed the nurses' station. Words were spoken to him, but they didn't register. The rush of the elevator transported him to the lobby where he stepped out onto the sidewalk. The fresh air felt more like a slap to his face than the welcome breeze that it was. Not wanting to go back to the office, and unable to think, his legs carried him down the Embarcadero to a bench that overlooked the San Francisco Bay. He watched as the ferries came and went, wishing he had had the chance to take Sylvia for a ride on one. She had been too sick when she arrived to do anything like that.

It wasn't until dark when Jack finally gathered the energy to stand. *What does one do when they lose both parents?* He didn't know the answer, nor did he know what to do with himself, so he walked the streets, meandering from one to another. He couldn't blame God for his losses. Sylvia outlived Jack's father by over three decades. He couldn't blame himself, other than for leaving the small town after high school and not being there for her all of these years. She had wanted him to make something of himself and was so proud of all he had accomplished. There was no one to blame for Sylvia's death, but that didn't lessen the grief. In fact, it almost made it worse because he couldn't be angry, only engulfed in sadness.

Jack's feet took him down blocks where he had never ventured before. He was only paying half-attention to the street names and his surroundings. Occasionally, music belted out of an apartment or an establishment, but only for the moment he passed by. The smell of pot caught his nose more than once. But, it was the fog nearly dripping on the tip of his nose that was constant. It had thickened greatly in the past hour.

"Hey, honey. How about a good time?"

Jack looked up and became face-to-face with a taller than average Asian woman. Her high heels had to be five inches and were candy apple red. Fishnet stockings wrapped her legs like a fisherman's net on his catch of the day. Jack had never thought of fishnets that way before. Her freshly manicured nails reached out and touched him under his chin.

"What's the matter with my new friend?" she asked.

"You ever lose everyone that meant something to you?" he asked.

"Sure have, honey. That's why I make people feel better now. I know what it's like to lose." She snuffed out her cigarette on the sidewalk with the toe-tip of her right heel. "Come with me. I know a place we can talk."

Not knowing what else to do, but also fully aware of what she was offering, Jack let her take his hand and followed her.

"What's your name, honey?" she asked.

"Jack."

"Jack. I bet you get a lot of jokes with that name. Jack rabbit. You don't know Jack. Jack in the box. I'm sure they're endless. I'm Monique. We'll get you cheered up."

"I don't..."

"No worries. No pressure. Just talking." Monique smiled at him, her white teeth reflecting in the street lights.

Jack nodded and released his hand from hers, but kept following her. They turned two more blocks when a poster in a window caught his eye.

"Hold on," he said. Jack walked over to the window and stared at the photo in the poster. *Could it be?* His eyes lead him to beneath the photo, and there was the confirmation he what he already knew.

The poster read, "SAMANTHA SOUNDER, National Geographic Photographer, Exhibit Thursday, May 4th."

Samantha? Coming here? Next week? Jack noticed that she hadn't changed a bit since high school, except for a few age lines. She looked radiant.

"I need to go," he said.

Monique wrinkled her brow, but Jack was running down the sidewalk before she could figure out what to say. He had made a mental note of the gallery's name, Fog and Sand, and didn't stop running toward the bay until he reached his office several blocks later.

The office was dark and very quiet. He didn't bother turning on the lights as he sat in his leather chair and looked out the large glass window. The lights of San Francisco below combined with the thought of Samantha soothed him. He had no one to call. Normally he would have called his mother to tell him Samantha was coming to town, and what were the odds of that?

He spun his chair back to his desk and took his golden pen out of its holder. On the legal pad of paper, he wrote, "Samantha, May 4th. Fog and Sand." He couldn't recall the street name, but pulled the phone book out of his desk drawer and looked it up, noting the address and phone number beneath the gallery name.

May fourth was only a week away, but time didn't feel like it existed anymore. He wondered where Samantha lived now. *Was she still in New York?* He gathered she traveled a lot, seeing National Geographic next to her name assured him of that. He wasn't surprised she had reached such heights. Her work had always been stunning. Her soul connected with nature and it showed in her photographs.

It was after two o'clock in the morning when Jack left a note for Sarah on her desk and finally went home. Sleep came quickly, but so did waking up again only a few hours later. He had to remind himself that it was true. Sylvia died yesterday. He also had to remind himself that it was true. Samantha was coming to San Francisco next week. After the sound of sirens finished passing under his window, Jack fell back to sleep and this time didn't wake up until nearly nine o'clock.

There was only enough orange juice left in the refrigerator to fill half a glass. He loathed grocery shopping and sometimes asked Sarah to pick up a thing or two for him, allowing her a longer lunch hour, which she gladly agreed to. Wearing just striped boxers and a black t-shirt, Jack leaned against the counter with his arms crossed while waiting for the cinnamon raisin bagel to pop out of the toaster. The view from his sixth floor apartment allowed him peeks of the Bay, but it wasn't anything like his office view. Considering he was rarely home, he took convenience and cost over views. However, he did choose a two bedroom because he had always hoped that one day he would have a wife, and perhaps a child, to share his space with. Some days he blamed God for his loneliness and others he blamed work. It certainly could have gone either way. Sylvia had always worried that Jack wouldn't find someone to love.

"Jack, boy, you need a good woman in your life. Do you know how lonely I've been since I lost your father?" she'd say.

"Yes, Mom, I know." Jack didn't have to remind her of all the nights he listened to her tears between their bedroom walls. How she camouflaged her red eyes in the morning. Mostly, how she stared off at nothing during the rare times they ate dinner together, obviously thinking about him.

"Don't be too picky," she'd add. "There are plenty of nice women out there. I meet them in the diner all the time."

"I know you do, Mom." Jack didn't have a reason for being alone. He couldn't fathom why other than that he didn't put himself out there. He imagined a day when *she* would walk into his life and they would live happily ever after, and when he wasn't imagining that, he was working.

The popping bagel startled Jack. He pulled it from the toaster, not worrying about burning his fingers, and dropped the two halves on a plate. After spreading cream cheese on each half, he took his half glass of orange juice and the bagel on a plate to his kitchen table. Last Sunday's paper was still untouched. He opened the business section, but couldn't wrap his head around the words of the article. Fanning through the Arts & Leisure pages, the familiar poster, as an ad, showed itself a few pages in. It was a half-page ad that the gallery ran. Jack looked at Samantha's image again as he slowly and carefully tore the ad out of the paper and stuck it in his briefcase. He wasn't sure how she would feel about seeing him. He wondered if she was single. He wondered if she would recognize him as readily as he did her.

As he stuck the ad to his refrigerator, the phone rang.

"Hello?"

"Jack, it's me, Sarah. Are you okay? I got your note about your mother. I'm so sorry."

"Yes, I'm okay. Or at least I will be."

"Is there anything I can do? Phone calls I can make?"

"No. I'm going to call the funeral home today. She will be cremated, and I'll take her ashes home to spread. She would want it that way. Sal will want a service for her, too."

Sal. That's right. Jack needed to call him with the news. "Actually, Sarah, you can do me a favor. Can you look into a flight home to Pontiac? I need to find out when the ashes will be ready, but I'm guessing within the week."

"Sure. I'll do that. Call me if you think of anything else."

"I will. Thanks, Sarah." Jack hung up and dialed Sal at the diner. For several moments, there was only silence on the other end of the phone when Jack told him the news.

"Your mother. She was one of a kind. She had the best smile. All the customers came in for that smile," Sal finally said.

"Yes, that's true, Sal. So very true." Jack thought back to a time when he was about sixteen and was at the diner with Samantha. He noticed a man looking at his mother the way Jack looked at girls. It unnerved him, but he kept quiet and listened to the story Samantha was telling him while keeping one eye on the man.

"She was a good woman." Sal's voice brought Jack back to the present moment.

"I'll be back next week, Sal. Let the others know," Jack said. "We'll have a nice service for her."

It was then when Jack looked at his refrigerator and realized he'd likely be in Pontiac during Samantha's exhibit. He picked up the phone and called the funeral home to make arrangements for the cremation of his mother and then showered and dressed to stop by the office.

"Sarah, did you find out about flights?" Jack asked as he approached Sarah's desk.

"Yes, here's a list of some for next week. San Francisco to Chicago has a lot of options." Sarah handed him a piece of folded paper.

"Thank you. I'll need a rental car as well. I'll be in my office making calls."

Jack sat at his desk and pulled the legal pad closer to him so he could read the phone number for Fog and Sand that he had jotted down the night before. His fingers shook as he dialed the number, not certain what would come out of his mouth when the phone was answered.

"Fog and Sand Gallery. How may I help you?" a perky voice answered the phone.

"Yes, I'm calling about Samantha Sounder's exhibit next week."

"Oh, yes. It's sure to be delightful. Will you be attending the reception on Thursday?"

"That's why I'm calling. I'm an old friend of Samantha's. We've lost touch, but I wanted to surprise her by showing up. Problem is...well, I might not be able to make it." Jack didn't have it in him to tell the perky voice his mother had died. "I was wondering if you can tell me where she lives now? Is she local?"

"Oh, well, all I know is that she's coming from Jackson Hole. Her prints arrived today and they're gorgeous. I hope you can make the reception."

"Me, too. Thank you." Jack hung up. *Samantha was in Jackson Hole?* That was a far cry from New York City.

Samantha

2000

Robert's plane was on time, and her habit of always being at least a few minutes early was intact. Samantha checked her hair twice in the rear view mirror before leaving for the airport. She had her Tahoe washed and vacuumed the day before. She knew he hated a dirty vehicle, and while hers was normally clean, she had been on a photo shoot early that week and the spring mud had left its imprint.

Between its nearly 6,500 feet altitude and the mountainous backdrop, the Jackson Hole airport was a tricky one for pilots to fly into, but Robert had done it before. Samantha waited by the gate for his flight to deplane. She wore tall leather boots, jeans, and a tight light blue sweater with a down vest. The morning air was still chilly, though the sun bounced off the mountains, generating some warmth as it rose.

"Stick to the plan," Samantha said under her breath. The plan was to take Robert by the frame shop where they would spend the rest of the morning going over things and so he could meet Steve. Then she'd take him to the diner for lunch before going back to the shop for the afternoon. That would handle about seven hours of their twenty-four hours together before she hopped on the plane to San Francisco. It was the other seventeen hours she was worried about.

Robert was the fifth person to come through the gate doors and the only person to make Samantha's heart race. *Stick to the plan!*

"Don't you look amazing?" Robert said as he hugged her.

"And you. How was the flight?"

"It was an early one. May as well have been the red eye with as early as I had to get up. But, you're worth it."

"Thanks."

Samantha took the driver's seat while Robert loaded his luggage into the back and climbed into the passenger seat. "This place never gets ugly, does it?"

"No, it certainly doesn't."

"That's why you fit in so well here. When you first moved here, it made no sense to me, but now it makes all the sense in the world."

Samantha smiled. "The shop isn't far. We'll go there and I'll show you the ropes. You'll like Steve, and he knows more than I do, so you'll be in good hands."

"I'd rather be in your hands." Samantha glimpsed the twinkle in Robert's eye.

Stick to the plan.

Steve was behind the counter ringing up a customer when Samantha and Robert walked through the front door.

"Nice place," said Robert. He laid his hand on Samantha's shoulder, showing his approval, but not realizing the sensations shooting through her body. She instinctively leaned into his hand, ever so slightly, while pointing around the shop.

"Steve is basically in charge of everything in front. I order products, he puts them on the shelves."

"Who keeps track of inventory?" asked Robert. He walked over toward one of the walls to inspect some of the frames.

"We both do. No set-in-stone system. Not yet anyway. We work well together and haven't needed to lay down too many specifics. He's got a great eye for matching prints with mats and frames," said Samantha. As the customer left, she said, "Thank you for coming in," then turned to Steve. "Steve, this is Robert. Robert, this is Steve."

They shook hands while Robert eyed Steve up and down until he seemed satisfied that there was nothing going on between him and Samantha. Steve was thin, but good looking. Robert knew that Samantha was attracted to athletic or stocky men with large pectoral muscles, which he boasted despite hardly ever having to lift weights.

An hour later, Samantha felt convinced that Robert would be able to handle the shop and left to grab an early lunch.

"You must be starving," said Samantha.

"Yes, I could eat a horse, but I'm guessing that's not appropriate to say around these parts." Robert chuckled at his joke and reached for Samantha's hand as they walked side-by-side down the sidewalk. Her arm froze from the shoulder down when he clasped her fingers in his.

"There's a diner up the road; we can grab lunch there then get you settled at the house." Samantha led the way out the door and Robert followed, nodding a good-bye to Steve.

An hour later they walked into Samantha's home. Robert carrying his suitcase and a briefcase. He put them down in

104

Samantha's bedroom. She didn't fight it, even though she had changed the sheets in the guest room.

"The fridge is full, so hopefully you'll find everything you…"

Robert's hands laid on Samantha's shoulders. "I have what I want right here." He turned her around and kissed her.

Surrendering, *Stick to the plan* was shot to hell in the matter of one kiss. Robert pressed her up against the door frame to her bedroom and kissed her harder. Kicking off her shoes, they hit the floor in unison with his unzipped jeans. Scooped up in his arms, Samantha felt the strength in his biceps as he carried her to her bed. She was the type who made her bed every morning, even if she was leaving before dawn for a photo shoot. To her, an unmade bed was simply sloppy and she hated the sight of it. But, an unmade bed in the early afternoon had reason, and Robert showed her that reason multiple times over the next two hours.

"God, I missed you," he said, crumpled up in ball next to her. He reached over and wrapped his arm around her waist.

Samantha lay on her back, looking up at the ceiling, part cursing herself for having absolutely no restraint when it came to him and part reeling in post-sex fog and glory. Her mind reeled back and forth between wrong and right.

"You okay?" Robert asked, pulling her in closer.

"Yes, just thinking about the trip. Sorry, but it's a big exhibit and I'm nervous."

"It'll be great. You'll be great."

Samantha nodded and wiggled her way out of bed and to the kitchen for a glass of water.

Damn it.

She knew being with Robert would pull the old emotions back. It did every time. The intensity of their physical connection would never bring them to the place of love. It was what it was, but it hurt nonetheless. To have a once in a lifetime connection with someone that she hardly ever saw and that she knew didn't love her, and when she was honest with herself, she didn't love him either. Her heart had always belonged to Jack. Robert and her photography had just been a distraction all of these years, and whatever they shared sexually left her feeling alone afterwards. Feelings that made her think she should just stay alone because the alternative was a high followed by very deep and lasting lows.

When Samantha sat on the plane the next morning, she looked out the window and watched as the ground beneath her grew farther and farther away.

Jack

2000

Jack looked at the ad for Samantha's Fog and Sand's exhibition several times since his flight took off. Something about Samantha's face helped to ground him in the wake of his mother's passing. He couldn't believe he was missing her reception, but he had to take care of matters with his mother first. After the wheels of the plane touched down on the tarmac, Jack put the ad back in his briefcase.

Being back in Pontiac only reminded him more of Samantha. He hadn't been back often since moving to San Francisco. This trip would be closure between him and his hometown. All of the memories would be stored away, but he didn't think he'd ever be able to step foot on Pontiac's grounds again. The loss of his mother ensured that. There would be no reason to return.

Once inside the rental car, he drove over to his mother's house. The same one he grew up in. His room still had his twin bed against the far wall and the old desk he had given to the church all those years ago had been replaced with a bigger one when he was in high school. It sat near the window with a layer of dust evident as the sun illuminated the surface.

"Anyone home?" A man's voice called from the front door.

"Yes, upstairs," Jack called.

Moments after hearing footsteps on the stairs, Jack greeted Paul Knight.

"Thanks for coming by, Paul."

"Of course, Jack. So sorry to hear about Sylvia. She was our favorite waitress. Always took such good care of us. A real loss to the diner and the town."

"Thanks. I appreciate your words." Jack rubbed his hands together, awkwardly, as he looked around the room. "So, I guess we need to get this listed."

"Yes. I've prepared some comps for you to go over. I also arranged to have an estate sale for the things you don't want to keep. That way you don't have to worry about what to do with it all."

"Thanks. I'm only here for a few days, so we'll have to handle the rest by phone and such." Jack walked out of his room and down the hall to his mother's. Paul followed.

"I'm going to go through her room for a moment. Feel free to look around the rest of the house," Jack said.

"Sure, will do." Paul excused himself while Jack stood in front of his mother's dresser. The enormity of the situation crashed over him like a wave hitting the shore with a vengeance. Her jewelry box was centered in the middle, and when he reached out to open it, a flood of emotions came in a second wave. Inside, he pulled out the gold necklace with a heart. Greg had given it to her after their first date. His entire savings went into that necklace. Jack pulled it from the box and slid it into his pocket. She had no other jewelry to speak of, and only wore the necklace on special occasions.

"A waitress can't be bogged down in jewels," she used to say. But, Jack knew that she would have loved a pair of diamond earrings. His one regret is life was never buying a pair for her.

Jack finished going through Sylvia's belongings. It took over an hour and Paul had already left, promising to bring back a contract later that day. Jack put everything except the necklace, which he kept in his pocket, in a box and climbed back into the rented car. On the way to the diner to see Sal, he stopped at the Post Office and mailed the box to himself in San Francisco. All of the furniture would be sold or donated.

"Sal?" Jack called when he walked in the diner. It was three in the afternoon and between busy shifts.

"Jack? Is that you, son?" Sal came from the kitchen, wiping his hands on his apron. "Lord, look at you. Handsome as your mom always bragged about."

"Hi, Sal." Jack gave Sal a hug, absorbing his mother's energy through him. "Good to see you."

"You ready for tomorrow? The church will be crowded. I'm sure of that."

"Ready as I'll ever be."

Jack had flown in on Thursday night, the night of Samantha's reception. The service for his mother was Saturday, and he needed Friday to finalize arrangements. His flight home was set for early Monday morning. Surely, Samantha would be back in Jackson Hole by then. Even still, he sent flowers—anonymously—to the gallery with a card.

"Let me know how I can help," Sal said. "Oh, and I wanted you to have these." Sal disappeared into the kitchen for a moment and returned with Sylvia's apron and name tag. It was the sight of those that made Jack lose it. Sal hugged him, the apron and nametag between them. A few patrons looked at the two men, but no one said anything. To Jack and Sal, it didn't matter if anyone else was in the room as they mourned their loss.

On Friday night, Paul stopped by with a contract to list the house on the market. There was an addendum that he would handle the estate sale, taking fifteen percent commission on top of the estate management company's six percent. Jack didn't mind. He wanted other people to handle it. He had what he wanted from his childhood and from Sylvia's belongings. Handling the details would be too painful. Besides the fact that he had to get back to San Francisco. Work could only wait so long before things would start to slide.

"I'm sure it will sell quickly. A house with one owner in a great part of town, it'll go fast. We've got it priced right. The photos will show that it was well cared for..." Paul stopped talking. Jack was looking out the window, not paying attention.

"She loved this town. Never wanted to leave. Me? I couldn't wait to get out of here. That's the only thing we differed on. She was happy serving people, making their day, if only with a smile or a kind word and good food. It was enough for her. I don't know what would have been enough for me. I don't know what I would have become if I stayed or came back after college. Shit, probably be married now with a few kids. Mom always wanted me to find a nice girl. Get married. All of that. While all I could seem to do was chase my career. Don't get me wrong," Jack took a step closer to the window and sat on half of the ledge. "It's been worth it. I've got a great career. If it weren't for what I do, I wouldn't have been able to afford the care she had at the end. For what that was worth."

Paul nervously shuffled his feet. "I'm sorry, Jack. I know this must be so hard on you."

Jack turned and looked at him, almost as though he forgot Paul was there and was just talking to himself. "Thanks. Need anything else from me? Signed?"

"No, I think we're good. I'll keep you posted on things, and will certainly see you in the morning."

"Great. Thanks."

"Oh, Jack," Paul stopped in the doorway.

"Yeah?"

"What about her car? The Galaxy?" Paul gestured toward the driveway.

"Oh, I'm having that shipped to San Francisco. Going to have it restored. Already have a guy down in Monterey lined up to do the work." Jack smiled.

"That's great, Jack. Really great. Let me know if I can help with that, too. Would be glad to."

The screen door shut behind Paul, and moments later Jack heard the gravel kick up in the driveway. When peace followed, Jack took a deep breath and sat down on the couch in his mother's living room. He wondered how Samantha's exhibition went the night before and then wondered how he'd make it through his mother's service.

At ten o'clock Saturday morning, the organ began playing. Jack sat in the front row with Sal, Sal's wife, Mrs. Cooper, and John, Peter, and Chris. All three of them still lived and worked in Pontiac. Mrs. Cooper, who was a few years older than Sylvia, used a walker, which Chris set to the side after she hugged Jack and sat down next to him. She squeezed his hand, and he found comfort in the Cooper's presence. He hadn't been in touch with them much over the years—life can do that—but was grateful for the childhood they gave him and especially for them being there for him now.

"We just loved your mother, Jack. You know that," Mrs. Cooper said. "After you left for college, my boys checked on her

111

often, especially in the last few years. She was family. You're family."

"Thank you, Mrs. Cooper. That means a lot to me. I loved every minute of playing at your house growing up."

"Look at you now. Big-time CEO in San Francisco. Good for you, Jack."

Chris and his wife sat down on the other side of Jack. He had aged a bit more than Jack, mostly Chris's receding hairline gave away his age. His wife, Molly, was one of the cheerleaders in high school. Jack and Chris often double dated with Molly and Samantha. They spent summers at the drive-in movies and swimming in the river. Molly was still pretty, and Jack was about to ask if she had been in touch with Samantha over the years when the minister walked down the aisle with his Bible under his arm.

The minister spoke lovingly about Sylvia to the packed church. When it was Jack's turn to give the eulogy, he choked out his words while squeezing his mother's heart necklace in his hand. Sal spoke next, reiterating much of what Jack said and adding that she was a great waitress and how much she made the customers laugh. How he would miss her smile and her friendship.

After they left the church, Jack, Sal and his wife spread Sylvia's ashes by the river in a private ceremony. The same spot by the tire swing where Samantha had taken Jack's photo. A photo he never saw and a moment that was long forgotten. His focus was on his mother at the moment. After Sal and his wife left, Jack sat on the bank of the river in quiet until he nearly fell asleep in the sun.

Samantha

2000

"Congratulations, Samantha. 'Stunning' are the words we've been hearing all night." Glenn, the gallery owner shook Samantha's hand. They stood near her favorite image, the one which also drew the most attention. It was of the Mormon Row Moulton Barn. "We knew that would be a hit here the moment we saw it. You certainly captured it in a way no other photographer has before. Truly stunning, my dear."

"Thank you, Glenn. I felt it was a special image when I captured it. But, to see it on exhibit here is really something."

"Samantha?" The receptionist approached Glenn and Samantha with a dozen roses. "These came for you. There's a card." She placed the vase of red roses on the table next to Samantha.

"Well, those are beautiful! Let me let you read your card in private while I attend to the guests," Glenn said.

Samantha reached down and pulled the card from between the roses.

Samantha,

Congratulations on a wonderful evening. Wish I could have been there to celebrate with you.

Love,

Me

Samantha couldn't believe Robert sent such beautiful flowers. He had never done anything like that for her before. She ducked into the gallery's office and called Robert.

"How's it going there?" he asked before even saying hello.

"Great. The Mormon Row Moulton Barn image is a big hit," Samantha said.

"Have I seen that one?"

"It's on display in the shop, so you should have." Samantha had brought the roses in the office with her to keep them safe until she left for her hotel later that night. "By the way, thank you so much for the roses, they're beautiful."

"Roses? What roses?" Robert asked.

"The dozen red ones…" Samantha's stomach sank as Robert continued speaking.

"Sorry, Sam, didn't send any roses. You sure they're not from the gallery?"

"Oh, that could be. I'll check with Glenn. I just assum…"

"I'm sure they're beautiful. Enjoy the reception. You should probably get back out there, it's still early, right?"

"Yes, I just ducked in to call you real quick. Everything okay at the shop?" Samantha fought the cracking in her voice. The disappointment was palpable, but she couldn't let him know that. This was her night, and she owed it to herself to make the most of it.

"Yes, just fine. See you when you get back."

"Thanks. See you." Samantha hung up and squeezed her eyes closed in frustration.

Then who are the roses from? Love, Me?

She couldn't imagine any other possibilities, but curiosity overcame her as she walked back out on the floor where put a smile back on her face to match the light of her photographs.

"This Mormon Row Moulton Barn image is just spectacular, Samantha."

Jean Scott was a notable art critic in San Francisco. She wrote reviews for all the top publications and when she liked something, it often became the rage of San Francisco, trickling down the coast to LA and then around the country, often landing in international terrain as well. Jean stood next to Samantha with a glass of Napa red wine in one hand and her glasses in the other. The glasses were strategically placed in the cliché spot of the edge of her lip as she glanced the image on the wall before them.

"I have a wonderful framer in Jackson Hole. He knew just how to emphasize the colors. I don't know where I'd be without him," Samantha said. Then it dawned on her. Could the roses have been from Steve? No, they didn't have that kind of relationship. Or did he think they do? She pushed the thought aside and listened to Jean, not wanting to miss a word.

"Well, my review will be in the Chronicle in Sunday's Arts and Leisure section. I can assure you, and I rarely say this to an artist..." Jean looked around the room and lowered her voice. "You won't be disappointed." She winked at Samantha then raised her hand and called to a friend across the room.

Samantha looked up at the Mormon Row Moulton Barn photo, making her miss home and also wondering how far that image would reach beyond the walls of the gallery. It was a personal image to her, and no one would know why, but it still felt awkward letting it out into the world. Her photography was so personal to her on many levels, and when an image went out as publically as many of hers had, it felt like she was running naked in front of the camera for all to see. Her bared soul was hard for her to accept, but at the same time, what would her work be if it was only on the walls of her home? They were her children, and like any child, they had to go out into the world eventually. But, that thought didn't make it easier or make her feel less vulnerable, as though she was on display as much as her work was.

"Fabulous night, Samantha," Glenn said, handing her a glass of champagne. She accepted it and toasted him, but only took a sip. She was a lightweight when it came to drinking, conscious of keeping all of her faculties intact, especially in public. "So, who were the beautiful roses from?" he asked.

"A secret admirer, apparently," she said. "I'm not sure I'll ever know."

"Well, a beautiful woman such as yourself must have many admirers beyond your photography, but tonight, this reception definitely highlighted your talent and how your beautiful soul shows through your work. Congratulations again. I hear Jean will be writing a favorable review."

"Yes, she indicated so. I will be anxious and nervous to read it though."

"I'm certain it will be wonderful."

"Thanks, Glenn, for all you've done. This exhibition is just what I needed right now."

Samantha left with her bouquet of roses after all the guests were gone and Glenn was left with the staff to clean up. She promised she would stop by again before leaving town. Back at the

116

hotel, she changed into her nightgown and sat on the bed with the Chronicle searching for Jean's other art reviews. As she turned the large pages across the bed, an image and name caught her attention.

"Sylvia? No! It couldn't be," she said out loud. The obituary was brief and stated Jack as her sole survivor, that he was the CEO of Golden Gate Publications. Samantha picked up the phone book and looked up Golden Gate Publications. Their offices were four blocks from her hotel. The clock flashed 11:11 p.m. "Angel number," she whispered. She made the decision to go to the offices in the morning. It was Friday and she had planned on going down to Half Moon Bay for a photo shoot, but seeing Jack was more important.

Fog cupped San Francisco like a glove as Samantha walked out of the hotel's front door at just after nine the next morning. Wearing jeans and a navy blue turtleneck sweater, she was warm except for her hands and cheeks. They weren't used to the damp fog, but Jackson Hole had certainly made her more adept at handling cold weather.

The doors to Golden Gate Publications swung open as she approached. A short elevator ride took her to the floor where his office was and a smiling blonde woman greeted her.

"May I help you?"

"Yes, I'm looking for Jack. Jack Sampson." Samantha tried to hide the nervous tone in her voice, but didn't feel she was successful.

"Oh, I'm sorry. He's not here. Can I help you? I'm Sarah, his personal assistant."

He has a personal assistant? Of course he does.

117

"I'm a friend from home. I'm in town on business and heard about Sylvia. I wanted to pay my condolences. Is he..."

"He's back in Pontiac. The service is this weekend. Do you want to leave a note or a message? I'll be sure he gets it."

"Oh, no. That's okay. Can you give me his card though?" Samantha felt a kick in the pit of her stomach. The thought of Jack dealing with the loss of Sylvia was unthinkable. She knew what their connection was and couldn't imagine what he was going through.

"Sure, hold on."

Sarah returned a moment later with Jack's card and handed it to Samantha.

"How long are you in town? He'll be back on Monday," Sarah offered.

"I fly out on Sunday. I was here for an event and happened to see the obituary in the paper. I haven't seen Jack in years. How's he doing? I mean other than..."

"He's doing fine. Just fine. It's been a rough month, but he's getting by."

"Is he...did he ever get..."

"Married? No. Jack is as single as any guy I know. I shouldn't say this...we only just met...but I wish he would find a nice lady to settle down with. Someone who can take care of him. He's so sensitive. Such a good man." Sarah scanned the office to make sure no one overheard her. "I shouldn't say anything more, but I hope you can reach out to him. He could use some friends right now."

"Thank you, Sarah. I appreciate it. Do me a favor though, don't tell him I was here. I want to surprise him. Maybe I can come back or delay my return. Okay?"

"Oh, of course. Mums the word." Sarah giggled as she held her finger up to her lips as she walked back to her desk. Samantha could see that there would be nothing between Sarah and Jack other than a friendship and working relationship.

As Samantha pressed the button for the elevator, Sarah came rushing back. "Wait, ma'am?"

Samantha turned around. "Yes?"

"Are you Samantha? Samantha Sounder?"

"Yes, why?"

"You're the one Jack had me send roses to. The photographer?"

"Those were from Jack?"

"Yes, but don't tell him I told you. He wanted to be anonymous. You two seem to have that in common."

"Yes, I guess we do. Thanks for telling me. Mums the word, or roses." Samantha put her finger to her lips and stepped in the elevator.

The roses were from Jack? Now it all made sense.

Back in the hotel Samantha took the card out once again and re-read it.

Samantha,

Congratulations on a wonderful evening. Wish I could have been there to celebrate with you.

Love,

Me

It was already past noon in Pontiac, but she picked up the phone and called the only florist in town.

"Hello, Jacob's Ladder Florist."

"Hello, I'd like to send a bouquet of mums to the service for Sylvia Sampson."

"She must have been a wonderful lady. Lots of requests for flowers for her. What would you like the card to say?"

Jack,

I'm so sorry for your loss. I wish I could have been there with you.

Love,

Me

"Okay, they'll be delivered in the morning with the rest."

Samantha thought for a moment. "Ma'am?"

"Yes?"

"I'd actually like mine sent to the house instead. Is that okay?"

"Sure, honey. What's the address?"

Samantha had to only think for a moment to remember the address of the home she first fell in love in. The home up the road from the river they swam in. The home with the porch swing Jack used to push her in. The home where she first fell in love with photography by taking pictures of Jack.

She gave the address and her credit card to the woman and thanked her. After she hung up, she sat back on the bed in the hotel, thinking about Jack and all the years that had passed by since they last saw one another. The innocence they shared had been tainted by life's experiences. She was older and wiser, but would have traded both in to have those days back again, even if for an hour.

*****

Samantha stood under the hot water of the shower. After napping Friday afternoon for longer than she had napped in ages, she wanted to get an early start on Saturday. The notorious early morning fog in San Francisco Bay Area was lens candy to her and she was anxious to get out and capture it. She pulled together her camera bag and tripod and headed down to the lobby where a cab was waiting to take her to the Marin Headlands, dropping her off at the base of Mt. Tamalpais where she would hike and take photos most of the morning, if not into the afternoon.

While crossing the Golden Gate Bridge in the cab, Samantha looked at her watch. It was still early in Pontiac and she knew Jack would be facing a long day. She had clipped the obituary out of the Chronicle and folded it neatly in her purse. The picture of Sylvia was one she would recognize anywhere. She remembered what a sweet lady she was, always thoughtful of Samantha and treated her like family. Jack and Samantha often went into the diner for grilled cheese or burgers and fries and a milkshake. Sylvia waited on them and gave them their privacy at the same time. Samantha thought she was the greatest mother anyone could have. Her own mother was shallow and distant; she and Samantha never bonded. Alcohol kept them apart emotionally

121

and eventually physically. It was one of the reasons Samantha left for New York City right out of high school. Hiding behind the camera lens was ideal to her.

Now, as she glanced out toward the fog-filled bay, Samantha wondered where her mother was. They hadn't spoken in six years, and as far as Samantha was concerned, that was just fine with her. She knew her sister would call her if anything major happened, but also knew that would mean their mother was dead or dying. Most friends felt it was cold of Samantha to distance herself from her mother, but Samantha saw it as survival.

Twenty minutes later she found herself in Fairfax in the foothills of Mt. Tamalpais.

"Is this okay?" the driver asked.

"Yes, there's a trailhead right there. Thank you!" She handed the driver a fistful of cash that she had already pulled out, collected her camera and tripod, and climbed out of the cab. The hike led her through trails around the mountain and facing the Pacific Ocean. Several hundred photographs and as many burned calories later, Samantha felt she had captured what she came to capture. The sun had popped out, burning off the fog, and warmed up the trails. She passed enough people to know it was a Saturday, but not so many that it kept her from being able to work the images. The landscape before her was lured in by her camera lens and once the settings were set, and the shutter button released, magic happened. All the while, her thoughts were never far from Jack bidding farewell to Sylvia a few thousand miles away. Her heart broke for him, and it showed in the images—her soul always came through in her images and often the days when she was feeling deep hurt were the days she captured her most compelling images, such as the Mormon Row Moulton Barn one.

Jack

2000

Back at the house later that afternoon, Jack climbed the porch steps. By the screen door was a bouquet of flowers.

"More flowers?" he mumbled. They were beautiful mums, appropriate, he felt, but he wondered why they hadn't been sent to the church with the rest. He brought them inside and put them in a vase that he found in the cupboard before thinking to open the card.

Jack,

I'm so sorry for your loss. I wish I could have been there with you.

Love,

Me

It can't be? How would she know? Jack immediately knew the sender was Samantha by the wording in the note. He ran to the phone on the kitchen wall and dialed the office.

"Jack?" Sarah asked.

"Yes, I'm calling from my mom's phone."

"Everything okay? Did the service go well?"

123

"Yes, it was all lovely. Difficult, but lovely. But, that's not why I'm calling. Did someone call you about sending me flowers?"

"No. I mean no one that you wouldn't expect. Why?"

"Nothing. Was just curious. See you soon."

Jack hung up the phone, not wanting to dig deeper with Sarah. He would track down Samantha on his own. He took the steps two at a time up to his bedroom and picked up his briefcase from the floor and lay it on the bed. Inside was the ad for Fog and Sand. He looked closer and found the phone number and ran back downstairs to the kitchen phone.

"Fog and Sand, may I help you?"

"Um, yes, I'm trying to reach Samantha Sounder. She had a reception there Thursday night."

"Hold on, let me get Glenn for you."

Jack tried not to breathe too hard into the phone while he waited. He was out of breath from running downstairs and made a mental note to get back into running.

"This is Glenn. You're looking for Samantha?"

"Yes, this is a friend of hers. I missed her reception on Thursday night because I was out of town, but really need to reach her. Do you know where she's staying?"

"Wait, are you the secret admirer?"

"I don't know? Am I?"

"Did you send a dozen red roses the other night?"

"Yes. Guilty as charged," Jack admitted, hoping it would help to get the information he needed.

"Oh, no, not guilty. She loved them."

"Good. So, can you tell me where she's staying, if she's still in town?"

"The Fairmont, but I didn't tell you if she asks. Tell her Jean did." Glenn laughed and hung up the phone.

"Jean? Who's Jean?" Jack asked, but the phone call was already disconnected. He dialed information and asked to be connected to the Fairmont.

He paced as far as the phone cord would let him while the phone rang in Samantha's room. When she didn't answer, he dialed zero to get back to the hotel operator.

"Did Ms. Sounder check out already?"

"No, sir, she's here until Sunday. Would you like to leave a message?"

"No, that's okay. I'll call back in a while."

Jack hung up the phone, not believing that he was here in Pontiac while Samantha was in San Francisco. Somehow the thought of her, the memories, gave him inspiration to go through more of his mother's things and to start packing. He knew he couldn't leave all of it for the estate people and Paul. He started with the kitchen drawers and worked his way through the cabinets. Four hours and two garbage bags later, he had made it through the entire kitchen. He labeled piles of items on the counters for the estate people and took the rest out to the garbage. One bag had been saved for donating to Good Will, but the rest went into the trash.

After pouring himself a tall glass of cold, sweet tea, he sat in the swing on the porch. He knew that Samantha's family had moved away when she left for New York. They had always been transient and her two years in Pontiac were an extended stay for them. He wondered what brought her to Jackson Hole, but wasn't surprised she ended up there to absorb all of the photo opportunities. He wondered if she ever married, or even if she had children, though he doubted the latter since she had been determined in her career and was never overly fond of children the way most women were. She was starkly different than any other woman he'd met. Ferociously independent yet the softest, warmest woman he knew. He wondered if she was still that way, but gathered that she likely was. Most people don't change at the core, and Samantha would be least likely to be swayed into marriage and kids over her career. Not that she couldn't have both, but he knew her better than she knew herself back in high school. She wouldn't have settled down with someone unless he championed her independence. He hoped she was still that way. Still the same Samantha, only older and wiser as he had grown to be.

The sun set in the distance. Jack still had Sunday to get through. He planned on getting an early start going through the rest of the house. He tried the hotel one more time before going to bed, but once again there was no answer in Samantha's room. *Knowing her, she's out photographing the sunset.*

He put the mums on the nightstand next to his bed. It was weird for him to sleep in his twin bed again. Not only was he way too big for it, but the sheets were musty and the same ones as when he left for college. Certainly they had been washed over the years, but still, he had a hard time falling asleep and eventually took a blanket and the mums downstairs. With the mums on the coffee table, he took to the couch, turned on the television and fell asleep with noise in the background and the smell of mums in the air.

*****

126

The rap at the screen door early Sunday morning started Jack out of a deep sleep. The couch served as a better bed than his old bed had, but the sun streaming in through the window coupled with the rap on the screen door were a rude awakening. He stood in his boxers and t-shirt and ambled toward the door. Seeing that it was Paul, he wondered what time it was. The battery in the clock in the kitchen had died somewhere along the way, leaving the time set for 3:07, am or pm was unknown as it was an analog clock.

"Sorry to bother you so early, Jack." Paul stood outside with two cups of coffee. "I was heading to church but thought you might need a pick-me-up before tackling the house today?"

"Sure, Paul. Thanks. That's thoughtful of you. C'mon in." Jack pushed slightly at the screen door while Paul stuck a foot in to prop it open as he handed over one of the Styrofoam cups of coffee.

"Wow, you've been busy," Paul said as he walked into the kitchen.

"Yeah, I tackled a bit of it yesterday after the service. It was methodical and medicinal at the same time."

Jack took a sip of his coffee.

"Well, it looks good. Great progress. Let me get out of your way. Call me if you need anything." Paul nodded at Jack and let himself out the screen door.

"Thanks, Paul."

Jack climbed the stairs to his bedroom and decided it was as good as any of a room to start with. By late that afternoon he had gone through the entire house, accumulating seven large bags of garbage and dozens of labeled piles for the estate sale company. He hadn't found anything else he wanted to keep. In reality, his parents were very young when they parted and hadn't much money at all, so their belongings were limited to the love they shared. Sylvia spent the rest of her days at the diner, more worried about other people eating well than what she had at home. The sorrow that Jack felt at times for the life his mother had to lead was overwhelming. At the same time, she was a good woman and so many people loved her, as was evident at the service yesterday.

Sylvia's room was the last one Jack tackled. He couldn't bear to finalize going through everything, and intentionally saved her dresser for last. He pulled her underwear and stockings from the top drawer, and as he went to place them in a bag, he noticed a small white card. It was dated and tattered, but the lettering still legible. As he flipped it over, the words on the back read: *Sylvia, Buy something nice for you and Jack. Happy 4th of July, Jack and Family.*

In that moment, Jack lost it. He sat on Sylvia's bed, now cleared of sheets and blankets, and stared at the card. The kindness of Jack and Family that day had restored Sylvia's faith and also the Galaxy for the time being. The memories of driving to the garage that day and writing JACK SAMPSON on the back of the one dollar bill and the one hundred dollar bill flooded back, washing over him. He wondered where Jack and Family were and wished he could let them know the difference they had made in his mother's life that day. Today that one hundred dollars was a fraction of what was in Jack's bank account, but no dollar or one hundred dollar bill meant more to him since the two with his name boldly printed on them. He thought about how the one dollar bill was later found in the drawer of his desk and sent to the tithing basket at church. *How could he have forgotten it was in his desk all of those years?*

"I've never been so emotional in my life," Jack said when he called Sarah at home that evening. "I'll be back tomorrow night and in the office on Tuesday. It will be good to get back into the swing of things."

"Jack, I'm so sorry again for your loss. You've been through a lot. Take your time." Sarah always knew what to say whether it was to Jack or someone calling Golden Gate Publications.

"Thanks, Sarah, but I can't stay away forever. Time to get back to work. I'll see you Tuesday morning. Oh, and can you pick me up some orange juice? I'm sure I'm out at home."

"Sure. See you Tuesday."

Jack hung up the phone and dialed the Fairmont one last time to no avail. Figuring she was out with her camera every chance she got, he decided Samantha was certainly taking advantage of the surrounding photo opportunities. He didn't want to leave a message though. He only wanted to hear her voice. Something familiar, something kind.

Samantha

2000

As promised, inside the Arts & Leisure section of the San Francisco Chronicle Jean gushed over Samantha's work. The image of the Mormon Row Moulton Barn filled nearly half of the page with the review beneath it. Words like stunning, magical, notable female photographers, nostalgia, and iconic filled the article, which in turn filled Samantha with worthy pride. Validation was one of those things that she never needed, because she would do her photography regardless of recognition from others, but she welcomed it when it came to her.

She scooped up four copies of the Chronicle to take home with her; one of the pages would be framed for the shop, one would be sent to her favorite editor at National Geographic, and the other two she would keep at home.

Samantha made a quick call to the frame shop before leaving for the airport.

"Is everything going okay?" Samantha asked.

"Yes, everything is great. Busy weekend, so I think you'll be pleased with the receivables."

"Great. My flights are on time, so I'll see you later tonight," Samantha said.

"See you then."

Robert sounded good, and Samantha appreciated his help, but she knew it was going to be hard to face him that night when her plane landed. With Jack so heavily on her mind, it was pulling her attention away from the physical attraction to Robert. She simply couldn't be mentally with one and physically with the other.

The concierge at the Fairmont stepped outside to hail a cab for Samantha while she checked out. She was satisfied with the images she captured and looked forward to being home where she could not only process the photos, but also process what she was feeling about Jack. Part of her wanted to stay in San Francisco until Tuesday so she could see him, yet at the same time she knew she couldn't ask Robert to change his flights and stay a few more days, nor could she ask Steve to cover at the shop by himself. It would be unfair short notice, and she knew she had to get home.

"SFO please," Samantha instructed the cab driver. She took a double take in the rear view mirror and looked closer at the cab driver. She knew, consciously, that it wouldn't be Jack, but the Harry Chapin song, "Taxi," played in her head and for a moment she thought it just might be him. The ride from the Fairmont in Nob Hill to the San Francisco International Airport, where the cab driver let her out, was about a half an hour. When they arrived, the cabby lifted her bags out of the trunk and placed them on the sidewalk. Samantha handed him enough cash for the fare and a healthy tip.

As the plane lifted off the runway, Samantha finally fully understood the lyrics to the old Tony Bennett song about leaving his heart in San Francisco. She was caught off guard by her longing to see Jack as she looked down over the world-famous city where he would be the next day.

When the plane's wheels touched down in Jackson Hole, Samantha held her breath. Not because the flight was over, but because she now had to face Robert. She would feign exhaustion, which wouldn't be a stretch, but knew that there was no way she could have the sex with him that night, but that he would be wanting to, and on some level, expecting to.

"So, how'd it go?" Robert asked as she approached baggage claim where he was waiting for her. He gave her a light shoulder hug and pulled her into his chest.

"It was a good trip. The review in the Chronicle today was great, so I'm happy about that. She can be tough on artists." Samantha slung her camera bag over her shoulder; besides her purse, her camera bag never left her side.

"That's great news."

They walked over to the carrousel and waited as the bags passed by, one by one, each looking almost like the next until her bright green bag poked through and started coming toward them. Robert pulled it from the belt and they headed to her Tahoe, which he had parked in the short-term parking.

"Hungry?" he asked once settled in the vehicle.

"Dinner sounds great. Or did you already eat?" It was past eight p.m. and she hadn't expected him to wait for her. She also wanted to kill as much time away from the house—the bed—as possible.

"I had a late lunch. Figured we'd grab a bite."

For lack of interest in much else, they stopped at the diner. Blanche brought them menus, even though Samantha didn't need one. She knew what she wanted and looked out the window as people strolled by while Robert glanced over his menu. Lost in thoughts of Jack returning to San Francisco the next day, she wanted to hop on the next plane back.

Blanche returned and took their orders. Samantha was hungrier than she thought, and when the last French fry was eaten, Robert paid the tab, left a tip and they headed back to her Tahoe. She had been quiet over dinner, but Robert hadn't asked why.

"How were the photo ops?" he asked as she navigated the Tahoe back home.

"Good. I went to the Marin Headlands on Saturday. The fog was thick, but burned off. I'm excited to process what I got."

Robert carried her bags inside while she set her purse down on the kitchen counter and brought her camera bag into her office. She set it down next to her computer since the next step would be downloading the several hundred images to the hard drive then processing them in Photoshop.

"Coming to bed?" Robert stuck his head in her office door, but she was already staring at the computer screen, watching the files scroll by from her camera's memory stick to the folder labeled "San Francisco, May 2000." He walked over and put his hands on her shoulders, gently squeezing them, and she hoped he didn't feel her tighten them at his touch.

"Go ahead; I'll be there in a few."

"Okay."

"Oh, feel free to grab the review in the Chronicle from my purse. You'll like it," Samantha called over her shoulder as Robert walked down the hall.

"Will do. I'm sure it's great."

While the images downloaded, which was sure to take a few minutes at least, she went to the closet and pulled out the shoebox that held all of her letters from Jack. The photo was tucked in the frame of the New York City construction men photo along with the one dollar bill that had his name printed boldly on the back. Now she wished she hadn't done that. She wanted to look at the photo and the one dollar bill again. The photo hung on the wall above her desk, but she wouldn't dare to start taking it apart with Robert in the next room. Instead, she pulled out the letters. Sitting on the closet floor, she began reading.

Dear Samantha,

I hope New York is treating you well and that your camera is finding lots to photograph. I miss being on the other side of your lens...and holding hands and walking along the riverside. I know life has taken us in different directions for now, but know that I will find my way back to you. I promise.

Love,

Jack

Samantha made herself stop. She couldn't do this right now. Not with Robert down the hall. The letters were tucked back in the shoebox. After disconnecting her camera from the computer, she tucked it back in its bag, shut down the computer, and turned off the lights. She would process the photos tomorrow night after Robert was gone and after the shop closed.

Robert was asleep, as she had hoped he would be, when she climbed into her bed. She had been tempted to sleep in the guest room, but she didn't want to raise questions so blatantly. He was leaving in the morning, after all.

Sliding in under the sheets, Robert instinctively felt her and reached over. With his arm around her waist, he pulled her closer. She surrendered, pulled his hand to her lips and kissed it, then she fell asleep in Robert's arms, but thinking about Jack.

The next morning Samantha managed to wake up and head to the shower before Robert awoke. They had untangled somewhere during the night and with only two hours until his flight left, she rest assured that they would part without issue.

The hot water streamed down her back, washing away the lathered soap and shampoo. While she waited for the conditioner to do its job, the bathroom door opened.

"Good morning," Robert called.

"Good morning. Go ahead and start the coffee if you want some."

"I was hoping..."

"Your flight leaves in less than two hours. Better have some caffeine." Samantha quickly rinsed out the conditioner and stepped from the shower stall and into a large bath towel. Robert smiled at her and left to make coffee. She could smell it shortly after while she was blow drying her hair.

As she stood at her dresser deciding what to wear on this unusually warm spring day, Robert came in the room.

"Who is Sylvia Sampson?"

"What?" Samantha turned and faced Robert, shocked by his question.

"Sylvia Sampson? Her obituary was in your purse next to the Chronicle review. Did you know her?" Robert leaned into the doorframe, holding out the review for Samantha to see.

"Oh, yes. She was from a town I lived in during high school. I...well, her son, Jack was my high school sweetheart."

"Oh. I see. But, did you live in Pontiac? Why was this in the Chronicle?"

"Jack is a CEO in San Francisco. They must have run it since he's a prominent figure there." Samantha tried to keep her voice neutral. This was not the conversation she wanted to have with Robert the morning he was leaving.

"Did you see him while you were there? Jack?" Robert shifted his position in the doorframe and Samantha couldn't tell exactly what information he was fishing for.

"No, I didn't see him. He was home for..." Samantha stopped herself. She was giving Robert information that he didn't need. They weren't in a committed relationship and Jack's life was not his business. She felt her stomach tighten.

"Home? You mean in Pontiac?"

"Yes, Robert. Look, this is the last thing we need to be discussing. We've got to get you to the airport." Samantha pulled a top over her head to match the shorts she was already wearing.

"Is he why you didn't want to have sex last night?"

"What? What are you talking about? No. I was tired. It was a long flight, and..." Samantha paused, deciding whether or not she should say the rest of what she was thinking.

"And what?"

"Robert, why are you pushing me this morning?"

"Because you never don't want to have sex. I mean you've never refused me. What's going on?" Robert walked over and tossed Sylvia's obituary on the top of the dresser and looked down at Samantha.

"That's not true. There are lots of times I don't want to have sex. With you it just happens to be different. But, yes, I was caught off guard by Sylvia's passing and it brought up a lot of my past for me. Now can we drop it?"

"Sure. Whatever." Robert left the bedroom and went back down the hall.

"Robert," Samantha called to him, "I don't owe you any explanations." She wasn't sure if he heard her, as the words came out meeker than intended. She didn't want to hurt him and didn't want him knowing Jack was so heavily on her mind. But, it was true, she was avoiding Robert physically and that was new for them.

Half an hour later, Robert loaded his luggage in the back of the Tahoe and took his seat in the passenger's side. Samantha closed and locked the front door and climbed in the driver's seat. They hadn't spoken a word since he left the bedroom other than formalities about going to the airport. She intentionally stalled in the bathroom, taking longer than usual to do her hair and makeup, which needed extra attention to camouflage the damage her tears had done.

Unable to take the silence, and not wanting him to leave without some sort of resolution, Samantha finally spoke. "Don't be mad, Robert. I don't want the trip to end like this. Jack was a high school sweetheart. His father died when he was only four and Sylvia did a great job raising him. We spent a lot of time together at the diner she worked in or at their house. She was like a mother figure to me since my own was emotionally unavailable. Seeing her obituary took me back to a time in my life when I was truly happy. Most kids aren't happy in high school, but I was."

"Sounds idyllic," Robert said. He was looking out the window as the mountain scenery passed by. A moment later he spoke again. "What happened? Why didn't you and Jack work out?"

Samantha sighed and glanced at Robert. "For the same reason most high school sweethearts don't work out—because we were young. He went off to college in California and I moved to New York City for my photography. There really were no other options for us. We kept in touch for a while, but I haven't heard from him in years. And, no, I still haven't."

The Tahoe went back to being quiet until the sign for the airport came into view.

"Are you going to call him?" Robert asked.

"I don't know," Samantha lied. "Okay. Yes, I will probably call him." She hated lying, but left out the part about having stopped by Jack's office and talking to his secretary. It really wasn't something Robert needed to know.

"Look, Samantha, you're entitled to see whomever you want. I know that."

"Yes, we both know that all too well." The words came out more sarcastically than intended. Samantha made a conscious effort to change her tone. "Robert, there are times when I wish we were more than what we are, but every time we get together I am reminded why we're not. It just wouldn't work. No, I don't know if I'll see Jack again, but he and I had something special. Something different."

"Different is good. I get it."

Samantha was surprised by Robert's tone. She sped up slightly, hoping he wouldn't notice she was anxious to get to the airport, to end this conversation.

"Well, for what it's worth, you and I have something special and very different than most. I guess I just don't do 'normal' when it comes to relationships. It's something I'm coming to peace with. I've made a career for myself, and I love life as much as I can. It is tough not having any one person there to count on day and day out, but at the same time, I've learned how strong I am. It's a strength that I'm both proud of and saddened by on some level."

"I get it, Sam. I really do. In some ways I'm the same way, but I think you're stronger than me," Robert choked back the last few words. "I don't think we'd ever work because I know you don't need me. I need a woman who needs me. I hate to say that, but I think it's a lot of why we haven't worked out in a different way. I envy your strength. Your independence is admirable."

"Admirable? I don't know about that. It's just what it is. I don't think I can ever make myself *need* someone. But, that doesn't mean I don't *want* someone."

"Right. Well, I'm glad I came and was able to help. Remember, you *needed* me to come and help out at the shop." Robert finally turned and looked at her, but Samantha couldn't look back, not only because she was watching where she was driving, but because she couldn't bear to see the pain in his eyes or perhaps she didn't want him to see the pain in her eyes.

When they approached the curbside, Robert hopped out and grabbed his luggage from the back. As Samantha opened her door, he came around and stopped her from getting out.

"It's okay. Stay in the car." He leaned in and kissed her goodbye. "See ya, Sam."

"See ya," she said. "Let me know when you get home, okay?"

"Sure." Robert walked away without looking back over his shoulder.

"Geez," Samantha said under her breath, even though no one was around to hear her. A wave of sadness came over her. She didn't want things with Robert to be strained. Their friendship meant more to her than the physical relationship, and with that being strained now, she wasn't sure how things would be going forward. Their relationship had already been through so many bumps and blocks, but this time Robert was acting different.

As she drove away, she realized she forgot to thank him for covering for the shop. He was right. She needed him to cover for her, but she also knew that in a pinch Steve could handle it just fine.

Next door to the frame shop was a little gift shop. She ran inside and bought a Thank You card, wrote a note to Robert, and dropped it in the mailbox down the sidewalk before going in the shop.

"Welcome back!" Steve said when Samantha came through the door.

"Thank you! How'd it go?"

"Good, I guess," Steve said.

"You guess? Was everything with Robert okay?"

"Yes, but first tell me about the exhibition!" Steve came from behind the counter and gave Samantha a hug.

"It was incredible, Steve. Really great turnout and Jean Scott was there, the critic for the Chronicle. Look at this review she wrote." Samantha pulled the article gently out of her oversized purse. "I'd love it if you could frame it to hang in here? It gave me chills to read it."

"Let me read it before we frame it!" Steve took the article from Samantha and laid it out on the counter. While he read, Samantha went back to her office and put her purse under her desk and turned on her computer. Her phone's voicemail light was lit up, but she wanted to get back to Steve. Messages could wait.

"This is amazing, Samantha. I'm so proud of you!" Steve gave her another hug.

"Think you can frame it okay? I tried not to let it crease." Samantha spread her hands across the article to smooth it out some more.

"Sure. I'll get on it today," Steve said. "I knew they would love the barn shot. Who wouldn't? I've seen it come through here hundreds of times, but no one has ever captured it like this."

"Well, I think I have an advantage by living here. Most people are through for a few days or a week or two and have to take what they can get for lighting."

"You're being modest. But, you might have a point, too." Steve took the paper to the backroom where he began going through mats and frames.

Back in her office Samantha pressed the button to play her messages.

Jack

2000

Jack closed and locked the front door to his mother's house one last time. His luggage lay on the back seat of the rental car as he pulled slowly down the driveway, trying to take in each detail to store in his memory. The house and yard hadn't changed too much over the years, not the way they could have. Jack found out from the Coopers that the boys took turns going over to Sylvia's to do yard work and to fix things around the house when needed.

"She was a second mom to us, Jack," they told her over lunch on Sunday. He broke away from the house for a short bit when they called him and asked him to lunch. The truth was, he needed the break and it was good to catch up with them.

"I had no idea," Jack said.

"She didn't want you to worry about her," Chris said. "She knew you had big things going on out there in San Francisco and didn't want you worrying about coming back to take care of her."

"I would have, though." Jack said. "All she had to do was call."

"That's just it. She knew you would have. She knew you had more important things to do, though," Peter said.

"Nothing was more important than my momma. I wished she had told me she needed help," Jack said. "But, I should have known. She worked so much and there's no way she could do all the yard work needed."

"She was a good woman," Mrs. Cooper said. She patted Jack on the back.

"Thank you, all of you, for being so good to her."

They were at Sal's Diner even though the initial concern was that it would be too hard on Jack. But, he insisted because he had something he wanted to do while there.

"Can I get you anything else?" Sandra asked. She was Sal's new waitress who had started after Sylvia left for San Francisco.

"The check would be great. Thank you," Jack said. He then turned to the Coopers and said he was going to sit and enjoy a cup of coffee before going back to the house. They took the hint, said their good-byes and left.

"Here you go, Jack," Sandra said when she brought the bill back with Jack's credit card. "I just wanted to say that I'm sorry about your mom. I used to come in here all the time before working and she was my favorite waitress. It was her smile."

"Thank you, Sandra. That means a lot to me. She loved it here. I hope you do, too." Jack smiled at Sandra, noting that her smile was almost as bright as his mother's. "Could you grab me a cup of coffee to go? Black?"

"Sure, let me get that for you."

As Sandra walked away, Jack signed the credit card slip and pulled a one hundred dollar bill out of his wallet. He took the pen and wrote, "JACK SAMPSON" on the back. On the back of his business card he wrote, *Thank you, Sandra. Jack and Sylvia.* He tucked the signed slip, the hundred dollar bill, and his business card in the billfold before standing up. On the way out, Sandra handed him his coffee.

"Black, just like you wanted it," she said.

143

Jack winked at her and left Sal's Diner. As he drove down the driveway, he thought about how Sandra was probably sitting down in the booth he had just left staring at the one hundred dollar bill in disbelief.

"Now there are two one hundred dollar bills out there with JACK SAMPSON written on them," he said, out loud, as he drove to the airport.

After returning the rental car, Jack took the shuttle to the main terminal. While seated in the second row of the shuttle, he pulled out his itinerary. His flight went from Chicago directly back to San Francisco. By time the shuttle arrived at the main terminal, he had made up his mind.

"I'd like to change my flight, please." Jack stood at the counter, speaking to the agent. He handed her his itinerary.

"Where to?" the agent asked.

"Jane," Jack said, looking at her name tag, "I need to stop in Jackson Hole on my way back to San Francisco."

"Hold on one minute, sir."

Jack tapped his foot nervously against the base of the counter while he waited for Jane to search flights.

"Okay, looks like you'll have to go through Salt Lake City, but I can get you on the flight at twelve after eleven this morning. You'll connect in Salt Lake, then arrive in Jackson Hole at three this afternoon. Does that work?"

"Yes, that's great." Jack stopped tapping his toe and handed her his credit card.

Within a few minutes, Jane printed Jack's new boarding passes and ran his credit card. "Here you go, Mr. Sampson."

Jack thanked her and took his boarding passes. With his carry-on bag over his shoulder, he handed her his one bigger piece of luggage to check through.

"You're all set. Have a good flight," Jane said.

Jack had forty-five minutes until his flight, and with his boarding pass in hand, all he had to do was find his way to the gate. He wondered if he should call Samantha, but liked the idea of surprising her. His only problem was not knowing where exactly to find her in Jackson Hole, but surely some locals would know something about the beautiful photographer, and he knew just where to start asking.

When the plane touched down in Salt Lake City, he took a moment to call Sarah.

"What do you mean you're going to Jackson Hole?" Sarah asked.

"I have to find her, Sarah."

"You mean Samantha? The photographer?"

"Yes, her."

"I'm not supposed to tell you this, but under the circumstances..."

"What? What aren't you supposed to tell me?" Jack asked.

"That's what I'm trying to do, Jack. I'm trying to tell you."

"Sorry. Go ahead." Jack looked at his watch. Thirty five minutes until his flight.

"She was here," Sarah said. "Last week."

"Who? Samantha?" Jack's voice quivered. He looked outside at the planes taxiing in and out of gates. The mountains in the distance were snowcapped. He had never been to Salt Lake City, but even from the airport, he could see the draw to it and could only imagine how beautiful Jackson Hole would be.

"Yes, she came by on Friday. She asked me not to tell you, but since you're now going to find her, I wanted you to know."

"She was there at the office? Is that how she knew to send flowers?"

"So you got those?"

"Yes. You make good co-conspirators," Jack said, then thought for a moment. "Did she say anything about where she lives in Jackson Hole? Anything at all that will help me find her when I get there? Her number is unlisted...I tried."

"No, we only talked about Sylvia and sending flowers," Sarah said. "She's very pretty, Jack."

"Yes, and a very talented photographer," Jack smiled as he spoke, the first smile in at least a few days. "Look, I have to catch the next flight. I'll call when I can."

"Okay, and good luck!"

Jack hung up the phone and walked the several yards to the gate, arriving just as they began boarding. He had been assigned a window seat, despite normally wanting an aisle to accommodate his long legs. He liked stretching them out in the aisle when no one was walking down it.

He tuned out as the flight attendants went through their safety demonstration. His carry-on bag was tucked under the seat in front of him and once at altitude, he put his seat back as far as it would go, closed his eyes, and thought back to high school when he first met Samantha.

"What's your name?" Jack shyly asked.

"Samantha. Why?"

"Just wondering."

"Oh. Well, what's your name?"

"Jack. Jack Sampson." While they shook hands, Jack noticed a look in her eyes. It was telling in that she was trying to be tough, he could tell by her tone of voice, but her eyes were softer than her words. He was instantly intrigued and wanted to know more about the long legged, dark haired beauty he had just met outside the darkroom.

"Are you a photographer," he asked.

"Yes, you?"

"No, it's just an elective. I figured it would be an easy class for senior year." Jack reached out and touched the camera strapped over her shoulder. "What kind is it?"

"It's a Canon. Want to try it?" Samantha pulled the Canon off her shoulder and handed it to Jack. Once in his hands, he raised the lens and aimed it at Samantha. It was then when he took full notice of the look in her eyes and at the age of seventeen, he fell in love for the first and last time in his life.

"Prepare for landing." The pilot's words carried through the airplane.

Jack looked out the window at the snowcapped mountains and felt a rush. They were bigger and bolder than the ones in Salt Lake City, and he instantly fell in love with the area, before the plane even touched the tarmac...or perhaps it was because he knew Samantha was somewhere down there.

Samantha

2000

Samantha's efforts to promote the frame shop to tourists, encouraging them to drop off their prints to be framed there and shipped to them at home, was paying off. It especially showed on Monday mornings when the weekend travelers stopped in to drop off their prints for framing on their way out of town. She and Steve were busy handling orders from the moment they flipped the CLOSED sign to OPEN and right up until lunchtime. People brought in either prints of their own that they had printed locally or ones they bought in a tourist shop, but wasn't framed, only matted. Many of the local photographers had their works matted and for sale in a variety of sizes at shops around town. They restocked the store with more of the same or new images as they produced them. The prints were the bread and butter of the town.

When customers brought their images in, Samantha greeted them and discussed the logistical process, at which point she turned them over to Steve, who went over matting and framing options. They worked like a finely oiled machine, all gears moving.

It was nearly one o'clock when the last of three customers, who all came in at once around noon, left and no one else walked through the door. Samantha looked over at Steve, who was head deep into the last customer's order.

"That was a rush," said Samantha. She walked over to the front door and looked out at the street. It didn't look like anyone else was headed toward them, for the moment.

"It's great when it's busy like that. Makes the time go quickly." Steve looked up from the last order. "We've had busy Mondays before, but not like this morning. That ad is paying off."

"Well, Don really planted a lot of seeds in the tourists' industry here, besides having a long track record here." Samantha turned back toward Steve. "So, where shall we hang the Jean Scott review?" She glanced around the shop, looking for blank wall space, but being a frame shop, there really wasn't any, especially one large enough to accommodate a framed, full page newspaper article.

"It should go where everyone can see it, that's for sure," Steve said. "I'll finish framing it this afternoon if it quiets down a bit."

"Oh, Steve, take care of the customer orders first. It can wait," said Samantha.

"No, they can wait. It won't take me long. I already have the matting and frame figured out, I just need to finish. The customers are on plane rides home, they won't know anything about the time set aside for your article." Steve smiled and excused himself to the backroom.

Samantha walked around the shop, organizing items and straightening anything that was off-kilter. Her attempt to busy herself in order not to think about Robert partially worked, but only because when she wasn't thinking about him, she was thinking about Jack. She recalled her conversation with Sarah and knew he was flying home from Pontiac today, likely out of Chicago. She had been to Chicago once to teach a class in landscape photography. The course filled up instantly, and she enjoyed wearing her teacher's hat; however, she didn't make the extra drive down to Pontiac. When she left after high school, after saying goodbye to Jack, she knew she would never return, and she hadn't. Though the Institute had asked her back on several occasions, she resisted and made up excuses. They eventually stopped asking, and when she moved to Jackson Hole, she kept her address private, using a post office box for mail delivery. It wasn't that she didn't love the Institute and her experience; it was that she had a hard time being so close to Pontiac, the one place in her life where she was truly happy. She supposed she didn't want the magic to be tarnished if she returned. She knew people who had gone back to their hometowns and went away gripping about how much it had changed and they didn't recognize anyone or even any of the streets or buildings. She didn't know if Pontiac had changed that much, but she wanted to keep it a memory nonetheless.

"Here it is!" Steve came out of the backroom with the framed Jean Scott review. He held it up high so Samantha could get a good look at it.

"Steve, it's wonderful! You outdid yourself." Samantha walked over and held the bottom of the framed article with her hands while Steve gripped the top. "It's absolutely wonderful. Now, where did we decided to hang it?"

Steve laid the framed article on the floor and against the counter. "Hold on," he said, and went out the front door.

"Where are you..."

Steve came back in before Samantha could finish her sentence.

"Right there!" Steve pointed straight ahead to the wall behind the register. "It's where I first looked when I came in the door." He smiled at Samantha.

"Wait, let me see." Samantha stepped outside onto the sidewalk, closed the door for effect, and came back in. "By golly, you're right. It should go there!" she said and pointed to the same spot. "Perfect."

"Deal. I'll take down those frames and hang it right now." Steven went to the back and came back with a small step ladder, a hammer, and hook and nail, which were tucked between his teeth and lips.

"While you do that, I'm going to get lunch. Can I bring you something back?" asked Samantha.

"I brought a peanut butter sandwich, but an iced tea would be great." Steve was already up on the ladder taking down the three inch wide golden frames.

Samantha walked down the road to the diner. Though she sometimes drove, depending on weather and whether or not she was short on time, today was too nice of a spring day to spend it behind the wheel. The fresh air while she walked helped to clear her head of all things Robert. She tried not to replay their last fight, or conversation, in her head, but she couldn't help allowing some of the words slip into her consciousness. By time she arrived at the diner, she welcomed Blanche's chipper voice.

"Good afternoon, Samantha. Will it be the same today?"

"Yes, Blanche. Thank you." Samantha took a seat in the same booth where she and Don had first discussed her acquiring the frame shop. It had become her favorite booth and she sat there whenever possible.

"How was your trip to San Francisco? The reception, right?" Blanche brought her a glass of iced tea.

"It went really well. Seems surreal that it even happened now that I'm back here, but it's always good to come home." Samantha looked around the diner. Most of the faces were regulars, but scattered within were definite tourists. She could tell by their t-shirts, the gaudy ones, in her opinion, that only the tourists shops sold. No one who actually lived in Jackson Hole wore a t-shirt or sweatshirt advertising it. The local breweries had better t-shirts and hats, and sometimes you would see a local wearing those in support of their business or because they won it in some kind of contest. Most of the locals could drink the tourists under the table, and they loved showing them up. Samantha didn't go to the breweries often, mostly because she was up early on photo shoots, but when she did, a distinct line between locals and tourists was always drawn, sometimes quite literally, down the middle of the floor. For the most part, it was all in good fun, but the air thickened as the night's hours dropped to the single digits and blood alcohol levels rose. Those born and bred in Wyoming liked to let newcomers know their place. Sometimes the bouncers or bartenders had to get in the middle of a dispute, but each intuitively knew their places. It was known, but rarely spoken, that some repeat visitors grew on the locals, almost to the point of bonding.

"Here you go," Blanche said. "Can I get you anything else?"

"This is great right here," Samantha said. But, as Blanche started to walk away, she added, "Oh, wait. Steve wants me to bring him back an iced tea."

"Sure thing. I'll bring it with your check." Blanche made her way to a table of newcomers, clearly tourists because they sported their mountain-scape t-shirts.

Jack

2000

With luggage in hand, Jack stepped out into the sunshine and breathed in the fresh mountain air. He had spent very little time at any altitude and wondered how he would handle it. All he knew was to drink a lot of water and not to overdo it, but he wasn't there to ski or hike. He was there to find Samantha, yet he had no idea where she was or where he would stay. Rather than getting a taxi, because, for one thing, he wouldn't be able to tell the driver where to go, he rented a car and asked for a map.

Jack shut the trunk after putting his luggage in it, a habit from living in a city...hide valuables. He took another deep breath as he walked to the driver's side and climbed in. He could get used to the fresh mountain air, he thought.

The digital clock showed it was 4:07 p.m. With a few hours of daylight left, and assurance that he could get a hotel room at any point, he decided to head into town. The best place to start was in the local stores and restaurants.

Finding a parking spot was easier than expected. He stretched when he got out of the car and looked around at the variety of stores. As he watched people walk by in jeans and t-shirts, he immediately felt out of place. He hadn't expected to be diverting to Wyoming and still wore the suit he liked to travel in. He took off his jacket, leaving slacks, an Eddie Bauer button down shirt, and a pair of loafers, no socks. As he closed the car door, he caught his image in the window's reflection and instinctively finger-combed his hair. Clearly the plane ride messed it up more than he thought.

154

Deciding on the gift shop right in front of him, Jack walked in and began looking around.

"Good afternoon, may I help you?" A perky, brunette clerk approached him.

"I'm sure I look like I need help, huh?" Jack asked; she only smiled back. "I'm actually trying to find a long lost friend who lives here. Her name is Samantha. Samantha Sounder."

"Oh, I'm sorry. I'm new here myself. Came to help my grandparents out and just work here part-time. We mostly only get tourists in here, not the locals, anyway."

"I see. That makes sense. I'll try another store." Jack turned to leave.

"Oh, wait. I'd try the diner. It's two blocks down and one over. Blanche knows everyone."

"Blanche?" Jack turned and asked.

"Yes, she's the waitress there. I'm pretty sure she came with the place when they built it. She's great. If Samantha is in this town, Blanche will know her."

"Thank you, I appreciate the help." Jack stepped outside and chose to walk the few blocks to the diner. He passed by stores that locals likely frequented, but he had such a good feeling about the diner, and this Blanche woman, that he kept going.

Sure enough, two blocks down and one over, Jack found the diner. Since it was well past lunchtime and not quite dinnertime, it wasn't busy when he walked through the door. The bell above his head jingled and a woman looked up from behind the counter.

"Good afternoon. Take a seat anywhere you want and I'll bring you a menu," she said.

Jack stepped up to the counter and took a seat. He didn't like sitting in booths all by himself, but a counter was acceptable. He was hungry, having not eaten lunch on either flight. When Blanche came over to him, he read her nametag and knew he was in the right place.

"So, you're Blanche?" he said.

"Well, honey, that depends on who wants to know and why," she laughed. Jack was reminded of Sylvia. Blanche clearly charmed the customers in the same way Sylvia did. He could see why the clerk knew that Blanche would know everyone in town, because she was the kind of woman you wanted around you on a good day or bad.

"Ya know, Blanche, my mom was a waitress. Best one in all of Illinois, if not the whole eastern side of the United States."

"Well, I'll be darned." Blanche put a menu on the counter for Jack. "It's a tough job, people have no idea. But, I wouldn't do anything else."

"I hear you. She was the same way about it. It was her smile that brought the customers back in time and time again," Jack said.

"She passed, didn't she?" Blanche was more than just a pretty face, even if it was an aged pretty face."

"Yes, just had her service a few days ago," Jack said. He took a deep breath and looked up at the ceiling, away from Blanche's sympathetic eyes. After regaining some sense of strength and composure, he looked down at the menu.

"I'm sorry for your loss. Family is the hardest to lose, especially a mother." Blanche reached down and squeezed Jack's hand. "See what's on the menu that you like. Let me know if you have any questions."

A good waitress knew when to give a customer space. Blanche was a good waitress. When she returned a few minutes later, Jack ordered a double cheeseburger and fries, hold the pickle.

While he waited for his food, Jack watched Blanche wait on the few other customers. He had expected to just walk in and ask Blanche if she knew Samantha and where he could find her, but the instant he walked through the door, he felt like he was home. He wanted to pause and enjoy the atmosphere of the diner, to not rush the process, and decided that he would ask about Samantha when the time felt right. He was certain that his mother wouldn't have given out personal information to any stranger coming in and asking for it, unless that stranger had a badge and a warrant. So, he didn't want to put any kind of pressure on Blanche.

The double cheeseburger was delicious. It notably rivaled Sal's secret recipe, a recipe that Sylvia never did find out the ingredients to. Jack couldn't help but ask her while she was in the hospital.

"Oh, son, you know Sal kept that under lock and key," she had said.

In hindsight, Jack knew that had she known, she would have taken it to the grave with her.

With the jingle of the bell over the front door when each customer came or left, Jack instinctively looked to see if it was Samantha. He knew she loved grilled cheese and fries, at least back in high school, and no doubt spent time here. He wondered what booth she sat at. Whether or not she and Blanche talked beyond small talk. Whether or not Blanche reminded her of Sylvia in some ways. But, mostly, whether or not she had told Blanche about him.

"How about dessert?" Blanched asked from the other side of the counter. "Apple pie is delicious."

"Ya know, a small slice sounds just perfect." Jack pushed his plate aside and took a sip of his iced water. "Oh, Blanche, could you also pour me a cup of coffee? Black."

"Sure, sweetheart."

"It could be a late night, so I could use the caffeine."

"Where are you visiting from?" Blanche asked as she placed a slice of pie in front of Jack.

"San Francisco by way of Chicago," Jack said. "I went home for my mother's service." He stopped short of making up an excuse for stopping in Jackson Hole. He didn't want to lie and say something cliché about wanting to enjoy the mountain air.

"I've always wanted to visit San Francisco. Never seems like I can get the time off. But, the truth is, I'm too afraid to fly." Blanche turned the coffee cup that was in front of Jack over and poured it to almost the brim with black coffee.

"Flying isn't so bad, but these mountains can make it tricky. Did you grow up here?"

"Sure did. My daddy owned this diner until he died about ten years ago. Momma was a waitress, and she went shortly after he did. Funny, they couldn't stand being apart on earth, so I guess she couldn't stand him being gone. I was already working here, had been since I was a teen, so I inherited it. My husband, Jason, and I run it now. He's the cook."

"Well, that worked out okay, now didn't it?" Jack wiped a bit of apple off his chin. "This, by the way is delicious." He gestured at the pie.

"I thought you'd like it." Blanche smiled and left to wait on another table. Jack looked around the diner and noticed that the early dinner patrons were starting to come in. He assessed that if he was going to ask about Samantha, he should do it before the tables were full and Blanche was too busy.

As he ate the last bite of pie, Blanche came over and refilled his coffee cup.

"I bet you know the whole town, Blanche. No doubt everyone comes to see you like they did my momma." Jack picked up the coffee mug and took a sip.

"Yes, I reckon I know everyone, except the tourists, of course. But, we have a lot of repeat visitors to these parts. People come and go, but most want to come back again. You'll see, you'll come back." She winked at Jack.

"Yes, this is my first time here. I'm looking for a childhood friend, actually." Jack's face softened at the thought of Samantha. "She's a photographer. Maybe you know her?"

"Are you talking about Samantha? Samantha Sounder?" Blanche asked. The way she asked made Jack wonder if a lot of people came in asking about Samantha.

"Yes, that's her. You know her?"

"Of course. Beautiful woman like that with a big camera lens around her neck, she stands out. She's also a friend." Blanche leaned her elbows on the counter. "You just missed her though. She was in earlier for lunch, like she does just about every day if she's not out on a photo shoot or travel...hey, wait. She just came

159

back from San Francisco. Had some big exhibit there. She's big time, you know."

"Yes, I know. I saw the ad for the exhibit. I wanted to go, but I had to be in Illinois. Can you keep a secret?"

"I sure can, but you have to tell me your name first."

"Oh, I'm sorry. Jack. Jack Sampson from Pontiac, Illinois." Jack reached out and shook Blanche's hand.

"So you're Jack Sampson, huh?"

He was right. Samantha had mentioned him to Blanche. His heart began to race as he wondered what was said.

"Sure am. I hope that's good news because I'm about to ask you where I can find her." Jack turned on his sheepish grin, and Blanche responded in kind.

"Well, she certainly thinks the world of you. That much I know. What's the secret though? Tell me that first, and I'll tell you where the most beautiful photographer in town is." Jack was beginning to see why Blanche was the town's favorite waitress.

"The secret, which you may already know now that I think about it, is that Samantha and I were high school sweethearts. But, what you or Samantha don't know is the bigger secret."

"Yes, I knew that. So, tell me, Jack, what's the bigger secret?" Blanche whispered. She glanced around the diner for effect.

"You can't even tell Samantha. Promise?" Jack was enjoying the banter and was glad he chose to go this route with engaging Blanche in his search for Samantha.

"Okay, c'mon now...tell me."

"She is the love of my life. Nobody else has ever come close." Jack's words seemed to surprise himself even more than they did Blanche, who nodded, as though she expected those words. He, however, listened to the words flowing from his mouth, but his consciousness hadn't planned them. His original secret was that he and Samantha were high school sweethearts, but he hadn't expected to so readily divulge the rest. He knew it was true though. Samantha was the love of his life.

"Jack, my dear, that's a secret I can keep. She would want to hear it from you," Blanche winked at Jack.

"So, about that. Where can I find her? Please don't tell me she left town after lunch for a photo shoot in Africa."

"Actually, she's right up the street. She is the new owner of the frame shop. Don, the old owner, sold it to her a few months ago. She's doing great things with it."

"Really? She owns a frame shop? That's so Samantha on one hand, but not on the other. What's the name of it?"

"Simple, Jackson Hole Frame Shop. It's not far from here, but seeing as it's past five o'clock, she might be gone. If you're going to find her, you better get over there. Here, I'll draw you a little map."

Blanche turned over a paper menu and drew a map for Jack. It wasn't far, but she didn't want him getting lost.

"Thanks. I need to go back to my car first. It's the other way." Jack tucked the map in his pocket, and took a last sip of coffee. "I'll be back for breakfast, most likely. Have a good night, Blanche."

When Blanche turned to wait on another table, Jack left a fifty on the counter to cover his tab and for an extra tip.

The temperature had dropped about five degrees since he first arrived at the diner. The wind had picked up and a storm was brewing in the mountains in the distance. He made his way back to the rental car. After looking at his watch for the time, he jumped in the car and headed toward the frame shop.

Samantha

2000

Samantha picked up her purse from where she left it under the desk that morning. After a long and busy day of being back, she was ready to go home to her now quiet house, since Robert had left, kick up her feet and relax. She was excited to spend the evening processing and sorting through the photos from her trip. Although she had missed out on the trip to Half Moon Bay, she knew the trip to Mt. Tamalpais had been worth it.

When she walked out to the front of the store, Steve was closing out the cash register. Above him was the newly framed and hung Jean Scott review.

"It really looks great, Steve. Thank you, again," she said. She placed her purse on the counter and took a moment to look up at it again. The image of the barn was prominent enough in the article that it grabbed attention from under the glass. Anyone walking in and glancing up would notice it.

"Sure thing. Congrats again, and it's good to have you back."

"Oh, speaking of which, we never talked about Robert. Everything go okay with him," asked Samantha.

"Yes, he was fine. He's a bit quirky though. Some of the locals weren't quite sure what to make of his jokes...or at least what we thought were jokes."

Samantha laughed. "Yes, well, he has an odd sense of humor at times. I'm glad he was okay for you though. He can be a tad on the bossy side, but I was hoping that since he wasn't on his turf, he would temper it."

"He was cool. Don't worry. But, if you ever go away again, I'm sure I can handle things on my own."

"No doubt, Steve. It wasn't about not trusting you to do it, it was more about making sure it wasn't too much. When I asked Robert to come to help out, I was new to the shop. It just seemed like a good idea. Now I know better for both you and me." On that note, Samantha picked up her purse and headed toward the door.

"I'll finish up here. See you in the morning," Steve said. "Oh, and will I get to frame some new images from your trip?"

Samantha had one hand on the door knob when she turned back to Steve. "Yes, I bet you will. I think I got some good fog and tree shots."

"Great. Can't wait to see them. Good night." Steve took the stepladder and headed to the back of the store.

Samantha closed the door behind her after turning the OPEN sign to CLOSED. As she climbed into the Tahoe, she instinctively checked her makeup in the mirror, then laughed to herself. "Not like I have a date tonight," she whispered.

*****

"Hello? Is anyone here?" Jack called after stepping inside the frame shop. The door was still unlocked even though the closed sign had been turned.

"Yes, back here. Hold on." Steve came back to the front of the store. "Can I help you?"

"I'm looking for Samantha. Is she here?" Jack was surprised to have a man come out from the backroom. It hadn't crossed his mind that she could have a male working for her. Or was he more?

"Oh, you just missed her. Is there something I can help you with?" Steve eyed Jack up and down, but Jack didn't look suspicious.

"I'm a friend visiting from out of town. Was hoping to catch her before she left." Jack looked around the store. "Nice shop, by the way. Are you her partner?"

"Oh, no. I'm the guy who gets to frame everything. She runs the place though. Steve. And you are?"

"Jack Sampson." Jack put his hand out to shake Steve's.

"Nice to meet you. You can probably reach her..." Steve paused for a moment. "Wait. Did you say you're Jack Sampson?"

"Yes, why?" Jack was starting to wonder if everyone in town knew who he was.

"You're the one dollar bill..."

Right as Samantha walked in the door, Steve froze his words.

"Dang it!" she exclaimed as she opened the door to the shop. The bell jingling overhead caused Steve and Jack to turn around.

"Forget something?" Steve asked.

Before noticing Jack, Samantha said, "Yes, can you get that envelope on my desk for me? The one from the Chamber of Commerce? I meant to take it home to review."

"Sure. Hold on."

As Steve retreated to the back of the store, Samantha glanced over at Jack.

"Hello," she said as she made room in her purse for the letter.

"Samantha?"

Samantha looked closer. *No. It couldn't be.*

But it was.

"Jack? Wha—"

Jack stepped forward and pulled her into him, squeezing the rest of her sentence out of her breath. "Yes, it's me."

Steve came back into the front. "Oh, sorry," he said.

"That's okay," Samantha said to Steve. "You can leave the letter on the counter. I'll lock up."

"Sure thing, Samantha. Jack, nice to meet you." Steve excused himself.

"Likewise," Jack said.

Once the door closed behind Steve, Jack tightened his hug around Samantha. He hadn't realized how badly he needed that hug nor how much he missed her. The warmth of her body against his sent sensations he hadn't experience in a very long time.

"So," Samantha said, but did not pull away. She looked up at Jack. "What bring you to this neck of the woods, literally?"

"You and only you." Jack loosened his arms, which now lay loosely around her waist so he could look more boldly into her eyes. "I was shocked to receive the mums from you. I tried calling the hotel in San Francisco, but you were always out."

"I went on a lot of photo shoots," Samantha said.

"There's so much going through my head right now. Can we go somewhere to talk? Let you close up here?"

"Absolutely. Do you have a car?"

"Yes, rented one at the airport."

"Great. Just follow me back to my house. It's about ten minutes from here, but no traffic."

Once out of town, the road to Samantha's wound briefly up a mountain. Jack stayed close to her vehicle, absorbing the idea that Samantha was in front of him. She drove on the slower side to make sure he could navigate now that the sun was starting to set and the unfamiliar roads were sure to be a bit daunting to a city man.

"This is my humble abode." Samantha unlocked the front door and lead Jack into her home. It was clearly a photographer's home with her enlarged images displayed prominently on the walls. The furniture was a blend of classic and rustic, something only a woman like Samantha could pull off. The walls throughout were painted in muted tones of blues, greens, and grays so that the images popped rather than the walls competing with them.

"It's a great home, Samantha. Certainly better than my condo in San Francisco."

"You have a condo?" Samantha couldn't imagine Jack living in a condo, let alone in a city. She never expected him to become the corporate CEO that he was. She watched as he walked around the living room, looking at books on the coffee table and photos on the end tables.

"Where was this taken?" Jack held up a photo of Samantha with another photographer. A beautiful mountain view was over their shoulders.

"The Alps. Probably about fifteen years ago. That photographer, Jeremy, was a good friend. I haven't seen him in a long while though. That's the thing about being a National Geographic photographer, you travel so much and meet so many people, but it feels like nothing is stagnant. I guess because it isn't." Samantha walked over and picked up another photo of her with a photographer in Iceland. "See this one? That's Ryan. He was a fantastic photographer. Died while on an assignment in Africa. I never got the full story, but it's amazing how it hits you even though it was someone I only knew briefly, he was extended family."

"I'm sorry to hear that. I can't imagine having traveled as much as you have, but I'm not surprised that this is what you've been doing all these years. It's always been who you are. Even in high school, I knew you'd go out into the world and do amazing things while I sat behind a desk somewhere dreaming of possibilities." Jack put the photo back to where it was. "I bet you don't have a regret in the world."

"I wouldn't say that. However, yes, I'm proud of where I'm at with my work. The grass isn't always greener, it's just different. It's hard to build relationships when you're always on the move, and the ones I've had...friends or otherwise...never solidified because I was always on the next plane out." Samantha walked over to the entryway and hung up her jacket. "Can I get you a glass of wine? Something else?"

168

"Wine would be great if it's red. White gives me a headache."

Jack followed her into the kitchen.

"Red it is."

Samantha pulled down two wine glasses and a bottle of Shafer. Jack opened the bottle and poured the glasses before following Samantha back to the living room where they took a seat on the couch.

"I didn't think to ask, are you hungry?" Samantha started to stand again.

"Oh, no. I actually ate at the diner. Met your friend Blanche." Jack lifted his glass to toast. "To old times."

"To old times," Samantha said as they clinked glasses. "And, to Sylvia. The best waitress and mom anyone could have asked for." Samantha smiled, wanting to be strong for Jack.

"Yes, to Mom." Jack took a sip of wine. "I don't know how the time went by so fast. I never thought I'd face the day when I'd lose her. Not this soon," said Jack.

"Time goes by so quickly. Just think of all the years that slipped by since we've seen one another, and now here you are...in my home in Jackson Hole. It's crazy," Samantha hadn't been able to take her eyes off of Jack since they sat down. "It's good to see you. I've missed you."

"I hadn't realized how much until I saw you in the frame shop. I've been so numb lately, losing Mom and all. But, when I saw you, I realized how numb I've been for a very long time. It's making me realize a lot about my life. About what I let go."

Samantha knew he meant her.

"I've let myself be numb in ways, too. You can't do what I do without some form of self-preservation. Meeting people along the way, but not wanting to get too close because I knew when the next assignment came along I'd be gone again. The sad part is, I was always happier getting on that plane for the next adventure than I ever thought I'd be settling down with someone."

Jack took a long sip of wine and watched Samantha's mouth as she talked. He had missed that mouth. Not only was it perfect, but the words that always came out of it reflected deep thoughts that expressed her emotional maturity beyond most women he'd met. Even as a teenager, Samantha acted well beyond her years.

"So, there hasn't been anyone? You never got married?" Jack prepared himself for the answer. As much as he wanted to know, he didn't want to know.

"No, never married. Not even close. But, there is one guy. His name is Robert," Samantha started, but wasn't sure how to explain her situation with Robert to anyone, let alone Jack. "He's more than a friend, but we're not in a relationship. I don't know how else to describe it."

"Does he live here?" Jack asked.

"No, back east. I don't see him often, and when I do, I'm reminded why we're not in a real relationship, if there even is such a thing." Samantha put her glass down on the coffee table and pulled herself in, closer to Jack. He wrapped his arm around her, guiding her body against his. "What about you? No one special in your life? Hard to believe, a handsome and successful guy like you."

"No, not lately. I've dated over the years, but that old cliché of being caught up in my work always applied. Once I got promoted at Golden Gate Publications, I really dove into work."

Jack looked down at Samantha and kissed the top of her head. "Do you still use the same shampoo?"

"What? No! But, that's funny." Samantha gently elbowed him in the ribs. "I used some strawberry smelling stuff back then."

"Well, your hair smells good."

"Are you trying to change the subject, Mr. Sampson?"

Just then, Samantha jumped up from the couch, releasing herself from Jack's arms.

"Where are you going?" he asked.

"I just remembered something. Stay right here. Grab more wine if you want. Or bring the bottle out here. I'll be back in a moment."

Samantha hurried down the hallway to her office where the photo of the New York City construction workers hung. She pulled it down off the wall and debated slicing the paper in the office or bringing the entire framed image out into the living room to have Jack help her. Opting for the latter, she made her way down the hall, carrying the large frame.

"What do you have there?" Jack asked. He had just set the bottle of wine down on the table and refilled their glasses.

"This is a photo of some New York City construction workers that I took that first summer I moved up there."

"Wow, let me look closer." After moving the wine bottle and glasses to an end table, Jack helped her lay the frame down on the coffee table. "Look at these guys. I'll bet they loved having a beautiful woman photograph them," he said.

"Well, I wasn't quite a woman yet. Just out of high school and scared to death to be in a big city, let alone New York. But, it was a wonderful time there. I struggled, but once I broke through, I never looked back." Samantha ran her hand lightly over the glass and across the men's faces. She never knew their names, but they had always been a big part of her life, her career. When the going got tough, and it did, she took out this photo and remembered the men who let her photograph them. "They were great men who did a nice thing for a budding artist. They'll never know what an impact they had on me over the years."

"That's a great shot. I can see why it means so much to you."

"There's more."

"What do you mean?" Jack raised an eyebrow at Samantha.

"Help me turn it over, careful of the glass."

Jack and Samantha gently turned the frame face down on the table.

"Wait one more minute," Samantha said.

She excused herself and went back to the office, returning with a sharp-edged blade.

"What's going on?" Jack looked quizzically at her. "Should I be worried?" he laughed.

"No, you'll like this." Samantha stood over the frame. "You'll like it a lot, actually."

Jack watched closely as she gently sliced the brown paper. As she peeled back the paper, his eyes grew wide.

"That's me on the rope swing. The one over the river!" Stunned, Jack leaned in to look closer at the photo. "I remember that so vividly. You looked stunning standing there with your camera, I was careful not to splash you."

"There's more."

"Huh? More? Is this Christmas or something?" Jack reached over and placed his hand on the small of her back.

"Hold on." Samantha gently removed the photo of Jack and handed it to him before carefully peeling away more of the paper. She paused for effect, and at the last moment said, "Close your eyes."

"Okay, they're closed. Promise," Jack said. Samantha couldn't see his face, but she trusted him. She always had.

As she nervously, but carefully, peeled away more of the paper, the one dollar bill with JACK SAMPSON written across it came into view. When it was completely visible, she sat down on the couch next to him and said, "Okay, you can open your eyes now."

Jack's eyes opened. And then they opened wider.

"How? How on earth?" He leaned over the table and peeled the one dollar bill from the back of the photo. Holding it up, he turned it around and looked at both sides. "In God We Trust."

"What?" Samantha was surprised by his reaction.

"That's what I asked the clerk at the candy store, I asked him why dollar bills have In God We Trust stamped on them. He didn't answer me, though. How on earth did you get this?"

"So, it is yours. I thought so, but obviously mostly hoped. I couldn't be sure, except the writing matched the old letters you sent me."

"You have those, too?"

"Of course, don't you?" Samantha looked at him closely.

"Yes, I do. I'm just surprised you kept yours with all the traveling, and, well, I don't know. But, still, how did you find this?" Jack sat there stunned to be holding his one dollar bill again.

"When I first started at the frame shop, someone came in and used it to pay for paint brushes, I think it was. When I saw your name, I...well, I don't know. I guess my gut thought it was you, but my heart went into protective mode, so I was never quite sure. I found the river photo in the shoebox when I went to look for handwriting samples, and well, I just had Steven put the two behind this when he reframed it for me. The original frame broke, so the timing seemed right. I figured it would preserve both of them."

Jack sat quietly for a moment and examined the bill before speaking. "Do you know what? I wrote my name on this bill so I could show the world that Jack Sampson trusts in God. The irony is, I haven't been that close to God since I left home. Again, I've just been too busy, I guess. No time for God or a woman in my life." Jack paused to regain composure. "But, the fact is, God brought you back to me even still."

"Jack, that's an incredible story. I never knew." Samantha put her arm around him and held him as he wept. She knew he was finally releasing the loss of Sylvia, that he finally felt a spiritual release. She let him cry, although softly, for several minutes. She didn't fuss over him, just held him. The tears flowed freely and deep sighs came and went until he finally looked up at her. "By God, how did he know? How did he work this despite my never praying or anything?"

"I guess it's what they say, God just knows best. But, I'm glad you put your name on the bill so I could find my way back to you."

"There was another bill. A one hundred dollar bill, actually." Jack looked at the ceiling pensively as he retold the details from 1976. "My momma, she got a tip from a wealthy family passing through. She couldn't believe someone left her a one hundred dollar tip, but I could. I knew she was that good of a waitress."

"What did she do with it?" Samantha picked up her glass of wine and took a sip as she listened to Jack. His voice sounded the same, just a little deeper since high school.

"She used it the next day to pay for new brakes in the Galaxy. It was the Fourth of July. We went to the fireworks that night and the next morning when she went to work and to drop me off at the Coopers, I wrote my name on that bill, too."

"Well, dang. Too bad I didn't find that one! A hundred bucks would buy me a nice filter or two."

Jack laughed and pulled Samantha in close to him. He kissed her on the head and said, "One dollar or one hundred dollars, you, darling, are priceless."

Samantha felt her heart melt right there in his hands. He was the same old Jack, and she felt exactly the same way with him now as she did in high school, madly in love.

Jack placed the dollar and the photo on the end table next to them. They sat in quiet for a long while, never leaving the other's arms. Inadvertently, they fell asleep on the couch, and it was well after midnight when Samantha woke up.

"Jack? You awake?"

Jack slowly opened his eyes, forgetting for a moment where he was. When he saw Samantha's face, he smiled. "Yes, I am now."

"Let's go to bed, it's late."

"So, I don't need to get a hotel room?"

Samantha laughed, "No, not tonight anyway."

She lead him down the hallway to her room. The same room, the same bed, Robert had just slept in the night before. But, this was different. This was Jack.

Samantha and Jack

2007

Stacks of cardboard boxes stood against the walls in the hallway, kitchen, and bedroom. A few more were at the office, but Sarah was going to ship those later. Jack looked out the window and down to the street where he saw the moving truck parking. Once they navigated the narrow street and turned on their flashers, three men climbed out of the truck. When the buzzer rang, Jack pressed the button that unlocked the door below and moments later they were coming through his door with dollies and padded blankets for the furniture. He was only taking his desk and a few other pieces.

"Jack?" the mover asked.

"Yes, come on in. As you can see, it's all pretty much ready to go." Jack gestured around the condo. "Not a large place, and the stacks are neat, so hopefully you'll be done quickly."

The three men walked through the condo to gauge the level of work needing to be done and where to start. Jack had taped and labeled every box, so there wasn't anything left for him to do except lock the condo when he left. His real estate agent would quickly sell it, as the market for his neighborhood was always booming.

"Okay, we'll start in the bedroom and work our way to the front." The movers worked swiftly, loading the dollies and taking two at a time with five boxes a piece down to the truck. Jack swept the bedroom while they worked the kitchen and then the kitchen while they worked the front room. He was anxious to get out of there, to leave San Francisco.

"Busy in here!" Samantha said. She walked through the door with a bag of bagels, a tub of cream cheese, and bottles of juice. "I figured they'd be hungry," she held them up.

Jack smiled, relaxing again. "I'll bet they are, but let's wait until the truck is loaded."

"Is that how you became CEO, by all work and no food until the job is done?" Samantha loved to tease him about his CEO position. She placed the bag of bagels on the counter and the juice and cream cheese in the fridge before going over to Jack and kissing him.

"Yes, in fact, it was how I became CEO, but since I'm not a CEO anymore, I don't have to withhold food." He reached into the bag and took out a raisin bagel. "Thank you for asking them to slice them, and for getting plastic forks for the cream cheese. All of the kitchen items are packed and loaded on the truck already. These guys work quickly and efficiently."

"Good, so we should be out of her by eleven or so?" she asked.

"That's the plan. We'll have a few hours before the flight. I just want to stop by the office and drop the key to the condo off with Sarah so the realtor can pick it up tomorrow." Jack wiped a drop of cream cheese off his cheek.

Forty-five minutes later the movers came into the kitchen to let Jack know they were done.

"Excellent! Thank you, guys. Help yourselves to bagels and juice. There's cream cheese, too."

Each of the men said thank you and reached for a bagel while Jack and Samantha walked through the condo. It certainly was empty. Jack's luggage for the trip was at the Fairmont where they had stayed for the past several nights since everything at the condo was packed up. There was nothing left to do except to throw out the garbage and lock up.

"Thank you, again," Jack said as the movers left. He and Samantha watched from the window as the truck pulled down the street. "See you in Jackson Hole, stuff!"

"I can't believe this is finally happening. It's been a long ten months." Samantha wrapped her arms around Jack. "But, we made it. Somehow, we made it."

"Jason is excited to take over as CEO. I know he'll bring fresh ideas to the company. I've already heard him and Sarah whispering about it. I think they thought I'd be offended or something, but I really don't care. I have everything I want right here." He kissed Samantha on the top of her head. "Are you ready to go?"

"Absolutely!"

Jack and Samantha left the condo one last time. She waited out on the sidewalk while Jack ran the key up to Sarah. A limousine waited around the corner, and the concierge at the hotel arranged for their bags to be put in it ahead of time.

"We're all set!" Jack said as he came out of Golden Gate Publications. He looked up at the building. "See ya, GGP! Thanks for the ride."

He and Samantha held hands as they walked the short block to the limousine. The driver opened the door for them and as they drove away, Jack didn't bother looking at the sights, he only wanted to look at Samantha.

"I never saw myself as a romantic, not until now." He put his arm around her.

When their plane took off two hours later, they looked down on the Bay Area. Samantha tried to grasp the idea that if it had not been for her exhibition there, nearly eleven months earlier, she likely never would have reconnected with Jack and now he was moving in with her in Jackson Hole. As the plane reached altitude, she held his hand tightly, allowing the reality to sink in.

The day after Jack arrived in Jackson Hole several months earlier, Samantha had given him the tour of the town. Now, they stopped in the diner to see Blanche, who clapped her hands together when she saw them walk through the door.

"This is the happiest I've ever seen you, Samantha," she declared.

"Shhhh, Blanche. Don't get his ego up," Samantha joked. She and Jack sat in the corner booth and talked until nearly dinnertime. She felt bad leaving Steve in the shop, but he insisted she take all the time she needed that day.

"Her service was amazing," Jack told her when she brought up Sylvia. "So many people there. Remember the Cooper brothers?" he asked, and she nodded yes. "They came with their mom. People who had been going to the diner for years or even for only a few months were there. She really did make an impact on people's lives just by serving them food. I wish I had that kind of influence on people. Instead, I sat behind a desk making sure magazines went out every month."

"She was wonderful, and she raised a great son. That I've never doubted. So, where did you spread her ashes?"

"You'll like this," Jack paused for a moment, thinking back to the afternoon he spent on the riverbank. It was hard for him to believe it was just a few days ago, and now he was sitting with Samantha. "I spread them in the river by the old rope swing."

"That's perfect, Jack. I'm sure she'd have wanted that."

Blanche kept bringing coffee refills to Jack and iced tea refills to Samantha, but didn't stick around to chat. Samantha appreciated the space she gave them.

When lunch turned into nearly dinnertime, they finally paid their tab and went by the frame shop to check on Steve.

"You two go enjoy yourselves. I'm fine here," Steve said.

"I owe you one," Samantha said as she and Jack left and got back into her Tahoe. He had returned his rental car that morning since he clearly wasn't going to need it anymore.

While driving back to Samantha's she asked, "How long are you planning on staying?"

"I hadn't thought about it. I didn't even know if I would find you. I mean, I figured I would, but you know..."

"Yeah, I know. Well, of course you're welcome to stay as long as you want to." The thought of Jack leaving when she just got him back was one she didn't want to entertain.

"I don't know what to say. Mostly, I didn't know what to expect when I got here. I guess we can play it by ear, but I will need to get back to the office..." Jack let the thought linger. He didn't want to wrap his head around the office in that moment. He didn't want to leave Samantha. "Let's think about it tomorrow. Right now I just want to relax and enjoy being together. Is that okay?"

"You bet," Samantha said. Blanche was right, she was happier than she'd been in a long time.

That night Jack and Samantha cooked dinner together and took a bottle of wine into the living room after eating. Between sips they took turns telling each other things about their lives since they were last together. By nearly midnight, Samantha started yawning.

"We should think about going to bed, huh?" Jack said.

"I'd say so. I should be at the shop in the morning, at least for a little bit. Do you want to stay here or go into town with me?"

"I may stay here and make some phone calls, if that's okay?" Jack stretched his arms over his head and Samantha stood and picked up the wine glasses.

"That's fine. I can come back and get you around lunchtime and then, and only then, we can decide about whether or not or when you want to go back..." she let her words trail off.

Jack picked up the wine bottle and followed her to the kitchen. "I'll do the dishes in the morning. Don't even think about them," he said.

"Do you know how long it's been since I've had a man do my dishes?" she asked.

"If that means anything other than what's in the kitchen sink, I don't want to know," Jack said. He took her hand and they walked down the hall to the bedroom.

The next morning the sun streamed in through the windows, waking Samantha. She rolled over and looked at Jack, who slept soundly between her and the wall. His face looked just like it did when he was seventeen when he slept, but when he was awake, the loss of Sylvia and the stress of years in a big city working his way up the ladder showed. A few gray hairs had sprouted around his temple, along with a few worry lines in his forehead. His cheeks were still smooth though, especially as he slept. At the core, he was still Jack though, and for that she was grateful. She fought the urge to think about the differences between having Jack in her bed compared to Robert, but she knew it wasn't fair to compare the two. She hadn't slept with Robert their last night together because of Jack, and now she hadn't slept with Jack since he arrived because, well, because he was Jack. He wouldn't do that. He would wait, just like he had in high school. There was never a hidden agenda with him, only love, and a lot of fun. Their days were filled with picking flowers, swimming in the river, throwing snowballs, and baking cookies while Sylvia was at the diner. They were the most youthful, innocent days of her life, and in many ways, she wanted to keep it that way for a while now that she had him back. Sex complicated her relationship with Robert, and without it, they had nothing. She knew in her heart that she and Jack would go there, at some point, but right now, the innocence of their love was being redefined and explored.

"I'm going to make some coffee for you," she said when she saw him begin to wake up. "I'll be right back."

"Mmmm." Jack rolled over on his side and stroked her arm with his finger tip. "Sounds good."

While Samantha waited for the coffee to brew, she looked out the window as the sun rose over the mountains. One thought that kept going through her head was what Jack had said about the dollar bill; that he wanted the world to know that he trusted God, but hadn't ever really talked to God. She knew there was a lesson in there, but never having been a spiritual person, she wrestled with the idea. All she knew was that a higher force of some undefined notion brought Jack back into her life, and now she didn't want to let him go again. But, his life was built in San Francisco and hers in Jackson Hole. They were two completely different places and their jobs both required their attention. Her heart sank at the thought, and her hand noticeably shook as she poured his coffee.

She knew from Blanche pouring him so many cups of coffee that he drank it black. When the coffee pot, which she only kept around for friends, was done brewing, she poured the coffee into a National Geographic mug and padded back down the hallway to the bedroom. Jack had just come out of the bathroom, and sat on the bed with his back up against the headboard and his long legs stretched out in front of him.

"Here you go!" Samantha handed him the mug. "I'm going to hop in the shower."

"Thank you. You knew I like it black."

"Yes, Blanche told me." She winked at him and went in the bathroom to shower.

"I'll be back at lunchtime. Make yourself at home and call the shop if you need anything."

Jack and Samantha stood in the kitchen where he was pouring a second cup of coffee and she was finishing the last bites of an English muffin and drops of orange juice.

"See you later," Jack said. He pulled her in for a hug and kissed her on top of her head.

After she drove down the driveway, Jack showered and changed before calling the office. He had updated Sarah only briefly the day before.

"So, when are you coming back?" she asked when he called that morning. "Wait? You are coming back, right?"

Jack laughed. "Yes, I'm not sure exactly when, but certainly this week. I know there's a lot waiting for me. But, I also really needed this."

"I know you do, Jack. You deserve it. I don't think you've ever taken a vacation day since I've worked here."

Sarah was right. Jack never had any reason to go on vacation, although he regretted not going home to see Sylvia more often than just the holidays. He tried not to think of that now. Guilt wasn't going to help the emotional healing he needed to do.

"We're going to figure things out this afternoon, so I'll let you know my plans once I know."

Sarah updated him on messages, mostly people calling with their condolences. The obituary made waves around San Francisco, and people Jack hadn't heard from in a long while called the office. He would start returning calls when he returned, but for now he didn't want to think about boarding a plane because that meant leaving Samantha.

He was sitting on her couch using the cordless phone to make his phone calls. From his vantage point, there were three of her photographs on the wall. Each one printed at at least twenty-four by sixteen, plus the matting and framing. The rich colors of her images were captivating and he could readily see why Jean Scott had given her such an outstanding review. He always knew she would go far with her photography, and deep down, he knew that was why he had to let her go when they graduated high school. Back then there really was no other choice, but on an emotional level, he knew it was the right thing to do. Neither of them, apparently, ever found the love they expected to, but they had both launched successful careers and he figured that had to count for something. All was not lost.

When he hung up the phone from his last call, he placed it on the coffee table. In the middle of the table was his one dollar bill. He couldn't help but to pick it up again. He traced the letters of his name with his finger. JACK SAMPSON. He shook his head in disbelief.

Just then, Samantha came through the front door. "I'm back!" she called.

Jack put the bill down on the table and stood to greet her. For the first time since he'd arrived in Jackson Hole, he gave her a long, welcoming kiss. With Samantha's arms around his waist, the kiss lingered for longer than it had since high school. It was then that he knew what he had to do.

"I've been thinking about my trip back to San Francisco," he said as he took a step back so he could look her in the eye.

"Oh yeah?" Samantha put her things down and followed Jack to the couch where they sat side-by-side. "What are you thinking because I don't know where to start. I have so many ideas running through my head."

"Well, I'm guessing we are on the same page here?"

Samantha nodded.

"So, I know I have to go back home, but..." Jack wasn't sure how to phrase the next words. His long pause made Samantha take his hand and squeeze it.

"If you're thinking what I'm thinking, I don't want you to go. But, I know you have to, so the question is...what do we do next?"

"Exactly. I am not willing to let you out of my life again. More than that, I know that dollar bill brought us back together for a reason." Jack said, confidently. He cleared his throat and said, "I want to be with you, Samantha. I don't have to move in here with you, I can rent a place somewhere in town or in the mountains, I don't care. I just know I want to be here with you."

"Jack, what about work? Can you leave?"

"Of course I can leave. I can afford to, anyway. There is always someone in the wings waiting for me to leave so they can position themselves for the coveted job of CEO. Frankly, it's overrated, and seeing you again made me realize how much was missing from my life. It's a cliché, I know, but at least I'm finding out now and not when I'm sixty-five and retiring."

"That's true. It's also why I've settled down here. I have a sense of family and community in this town that I haven't had since, well, since Pontiac. And, yes, I'm realizing how much I've missed out by not having someone by my side. I'm being spoiled by having you here. I want you here, Jack. Can we make this work?"

Jack wrapped his arms around Samantha and said, "We can make it work. This time, we'll make it work."

Samantha sighed deeply as she rested her head on his shoulder. She felt secure and comfortable in his arms, so much more so than when she was with Robert. She hadn't realized how shallow her relationship with Robert was until now. She put that thought in the back of her mind as she and Jack made plans to go into town to the diner.

"Blanche is going to be over the moon about this," she said.

"Oh yeah?"

"Let's just say she really likes you, and just as much, she likes seeing me happy."

Jack offered to drive as they left for town. "I have to get used to the drive, right?"

As they rode, it felt like they'd been doing that ride together for decades. Samantha looked out the window at the signs of spring as buds were starting to pop, especially as they descended toward town where the elevation was a little lower. They were different kinds of hills than what Jack was accustomed to in San Francisco, but he navigated them like a pro and when they arrived at the diner, they took their table in the corner. Blanche rushed over to serve them.

"What's new with the lovebirds today," she asked.

"Blanche, you better save this table for us every day for the rest of the days," Jack said. "And, keep the black coffee coming."

The next morning Jack flew home to San Francisco. Samantha offered him the one dollar bill to take with him, but he insisted she keep it safe at her place, knowing he would be back soon enough. As soon as he was home, they began making plans for her next visit to San Francisco. She could stop by the gallery since her exhibit was going for another few weeks. Steve assured her he could cover the shop just fine, and by mid-June she was on the plane to San Francisco.

It took until that fall before Golden Gate Publications found a new CEO. As it turned out Jack wasn't as easy to replace as he thought he would be. That meant every other weekend, Jack or Samantha flew to see the other. Once a CEO was found, Jack put his condo on the market. By then, they had determined that there was no need for him to rent his own place in Jackson Hole; he would move in with Samantha.

When their plane finally touched down in Jackson Hole, Jack let out a sigh of relief. It was a longer journey to arrive that day than either of them expected, but every step of the way had been worth it. That night as Samantha set herself loose in the kitchen to make them dinner, Jack sat on the couch. When the phone rang, Samantha answered and momentarily called to him, "Jack, it's for you. It's Paul."

"Hello?" Jack said.

"Jack, it's Paul. Good news, the counter was accepted. Your mother's house is sold."

Jack felt a combination of sorrow and closure. "That's good news, Paul. You can fax the papers here in the morning. When is the closing?"

"Thirty days. It's a cash offer. I think it's an investor and they will likely rebuild it."

"I don't want to know, Paul. Please just send the papers. Do I need to be there for closing?"

"No, we can handle it over the wires. You have a good night."

Jack hung up the phone. "Well, it's sold."

"At the risk of sounding like a therapist, how does that make you feel?" Samantha stepped into the living room, complete with apron and wooden spoon in her hand. Jack had a flashback to the days of making chocolate chip cookies in Pontiac.

"Part of me wonders if I should have kept it, but it just didn't make sense. It would have become a tumbled down place without proper maintenance. Besides, I have what I want from my past."

Samantha smiled and blew him a kiss from across the room. "Dinner is almost ready."

"I'll set the table."

As Jack stood, he spotted the one dollar bill on the end table. He thought about how the idea of ever seeing that bill again had never crossed his mind. He figured it would go through different hands over time and eventually go to dollar bill heaven. Only an act of God could bring it back to him, let alone through Samantha.

"In God We Trust," he said under his breath.

"What?" Samantha called from the kitchen.

"Nothing," Jack said. "Dinner smells good!"

They sat down for dinner, the most formal one since reconnecting, and toasted.

"To us!" Jack said.

"To us!" Samantha echoed.

Epilogue

2007

NEW YORK CITY:

"JACK SAMPSON?" The wiry old man held the one hundred dollar bill up to the light. The New York City bar was dark, and his scraped and tattered hands were as worn as the bill itself.

"What's that, Joe?"

"Nothing you need to worry about," Joe said. He tucked the bill in the back pocket of his jeans. "Order us another round, will you? My creaky bones need forgetting."

"Already told the waitress. You were too busy looking at that bill."

Joe waved a hand at his friend, indicating he'd heard enough.

"Remember when we built this damn place. It nearly killed me climbing on that scaffolding. It was my first time being that high up. Dang near scared me to death, that's for sure."

"Well, this here Smokey's Bar has worked out great for us. Lifetime of beer was a good negotiation for the extra work, my friend. I doubt they expected us to live this long!"

Joe laughed. "Ain't that the truth."

JACKSON HOLE:

Jack stood in Samantha's office deciding how he could squeeze his desk in next to hers. She was at the frame shop and wouldn't be home until later, and it was his goal to have the office set up by time she walked through the door. He didn't want her feeling like he was intruding on her space, but at the same time, they didn't want to turn the guest room into another office. She had it decorated so nicely, and they didn't know if they would ever have any visitors, but still wanted to keep it as a bedroom.

When the desk was finally pushed against the wall in the opposite corner, he felt satisfied that it would work there. It wasn't like they would both be in there at the same time most of the time anyway. He would use it during the day while she was at the shop and she would use it to process photos at night and on the weekends.

Jack leaned against his desk before bringing the chair in. The photo of the New York City construction workers was back hanging on the wall after Steve replaced the paper backing. Jack walked over to it and looked closely at it. He hadn't looked at it too much before since Samantha was quick to flip it over and cut the backing open. After that, it went back to the shop and he simply hadn't had the time to look closely at it until now.

"Smokey's Bar?" he laughed. "I hope you guys know that a famous photographer once took your photo."

THE END

About the Author

Heather Hummel is a novelist and a ghostwriter who has penned over a dozen books. By personal request from Arianna Huffington, Heather is a featured blogger in the Arts & Culture section of the Huffington Post. Her article titled "Why Agents Reject 96% of Author Submissions" gained remarkable attention in the industry, including ReTweets from *Publishers Weekly* and many quality literary agents.

Television, print, and radio coverage for her clients' books include: The Today Show and other regional shows; *Publishers Weekly*, *USA Today* and the *Washington Post*; and in magazines that include: *Health, Body & Soul, First,* and *Spry Living*, a combined circulation of nearly 20 million in print alone. A contributing author in *Successful eBook Publishing: The Complete How-to Guide for Creating and Launching Your Amazon Kindle eBook* by David Wogahn, Heather shares her wisdom in a chapter on ghostwriting.

Heather's second career is as a land and seascape photographer. Her work has been represented by Agora Gallery in the Chelsea District of New York City. A graduate with High Distinction from the University of Virginia, Heather holds a Bachelor of Interdisciplinary Studies degree with concentrations in English and Secondary Education.

Visit Heather at www.HeatherHummelAuthor.com

On Facebook as Heather Hummel (Fan Page) or Heather Hummel Photography

On Twitter as @HeatherHummel

Made in the USA
Charleston, SC
22 November 2015